SUBVERSO TERRAM

The Subverted Earth

By
Joel R. Webb

Dedication:

To my good friend David Smith, who has encouraged me throughout this journey. May he be richly blessed.

Chapter Index:

One: The Mausoleum
Two: Final Days of Terram
Three: Mt. Lithmer
Four: The Abominable Dream
Five: Char'gabble
Six: The Captive Existence
Seven: Loneliness
Eight: Rescue from Wolves
Nine: Discovery
Ten: Dry Bones
Eleven: The Hinderance
Twelve: A Place of Madness
Thirteen: Hector's Return
Fourteen: The Cackling Man
Fifteen: The Irrational Curse
Sixteen: Resisting Medicine
Seventeen: Gaven Post
Eighteen: Departed Friends
Nineteen: Feverfew
Twenty: The Strange Teacher
Twenty-one: Hemmed In
Twenty-two: Owl Head
Twenty-three: The Fall
Twenty-four: Leaving
Twenty-five: A New Name
Twenty-six: The Chase
Twenty-seven: The Light
Twenty-eight: Alman Freemont
Twenty-nine: Conversing

Thirty: The Servant
Thirty-one: Dregs
Thirty-two: The Devourer
Thirty-three: A walk with the Sisters
Thirty-Four: Letting Go
Thirty-Five: Avira's Song
Thirty-Six: The Pale queen
Thirty-seven: A Seething Pot
Thirty-eight: The Letter and the Chest
Thirty-nine: For Such a Time as This
Forty: Ameara's Plea
Forty-one: The March
Forty-two: The Casualty
Forty-three: Battle at the Gates
Conclusion

Chapter One:
The Mausoleum

In the early hours preceding dawn, the valley was asleep. Submersed in enchantment, it was a world hidden within a world. This was a place of mystery, even to those who called it home. Its inhabitants had learned to exist with the enigmas. They continued to dwell in utter ignorance of the forces ruling over them. Their souls were passive and forgetful, no longer aware of what had come before.

Below the sloping, azure peaks, the land rolled down in terraced folds. The wide basin of the valley was alive with growing green. Despite the frequent lack of sunlight, the grass flourished. It was a place of gardens and groves. The trees and shrubs thrived in abundance, fed by the mists which drifted down from the mountains. There had not been a dry season in over three hundred years.

At the center of this sleeping valley, tucked away behind walls of tangled growth, stood a mausoleum. Its walls were of white marble, strong, yet yellowed with age. It was a hexagon with six high walls and a sloping roof. There was no doorway. What lived inside was held in secret, hidden from ordinary eyes. Mortal force could not break through those walls. They were formed of more than stone.

If by some dread miracle of chance or fate, one was to gain entry into the sullen structure, they would find its interior lit with a luminous glow. The shelved walls and floor were clean-swept, without spot or blemish. The creatures which called it home did not produce waste, only subtle malice. They were more spirit than flesh.

There were five metaphysical beasts in all, each with its own ornate cage. They did not sleep, neither did they breathe, yet life lingered. It would always linger while there was purpose, a reason to wait. They would be set loose in due season, as they had been before. For now, however, their duty was to abide.

The first beast was a cat, an ocelot to be precise. This was a stealthy spirit, well-skilled in the art of guile. He could work his way into almost any place, given a weakness was found. His needle-like claws were sharp as steel and his ears could pick up on the slightest sound.

Beside the ocelot was housed a spirit in the form of an owl. The great bird was the size of a man. She was a watcher, a witness of many things. It was she who kept record of the sins of man that they might be recounted later to his shame. Her yellow eyes kept track of all that was. They peered past time, stone, and bone, testing the very fabric of nature. The broodish bird also held the power to evoke emotions as she wished. Her most favored pastime was the manipulation of men's minds.

The third entity was a wolf. His dark, shadowy coat hid the scars of many a battle. Deep within his belly burned an insatiable hunger. This spirit was the devourer, a consumer of all things. When set loose, he could eat up entire cities, civilizations even, leaving nothing in his wake.

The fourth creature was an immense snake. Long and undulating, the massive reptile lived to entangle and constrict. He too had a hunger, yet, the need to crush and cripple life outweighed the need to feed.

The fifth and final entity was a strange thing indeed. He bore the form of a tamandua with rusty red fur. The bizarre beast was a scholar. For millennia, he had studied the arts of reason and logic. His long, probing tongue was always testing the air for contention and doubt. This spirit had fed many a dispute and division, fueling many a false belief. His specialty was the justification of wrongs and the hardening of hearts and minds through rhetoric. Of all the caged beasts, he was perhaps the most prideful.

The competent creatures conversed together, biding their time. They awaited their next commission. It was the word of their master which bound them in that place and confined them, not the bars or marble walls. Had they permission, they would shatter these.

The spirits were not particularly restless, just eager to begin their work again. Their tasks of destruction were always the most pleasing. The memories of former triumph did little to sustain them. Nevertheless, each knew and was assured that it would not be long. The world to which their purposes leaned was teetering on the brink. A final cataclysm was near at hand.

The ceiling of the mausoleum was a gigantic clock. Inside its circular rim were five smaller clocks, one for each of the beasts. They kept time, beating out the years and hours. Their suspended pendulums like scythes swung two and fro, cutting away the time.

These clocks would chime out only when stopped. When they stopped, evil within would be loosed. Indeed, it would not be long at all. Time was growing short.

Chapter Two:
Final Days of Terram

In the world of Terram, all things were changing. The time had come when the consequences of spiritual rebellion, and the strife of man, had left this temporal realm in utter desolation. Most of the mighty cities had been destroyed by war or disaster. Creation was in upheaval, trembling in anticipation of a final reckoning. The lands were ravaged by storms and violent quakes, symptoms of unrest upon a higher level. Much of this place had become a desert. Nothing grew here anymore, not since the sun had been stolen away.

There was still a form of daylight, yet it held no warmth. It was chill and pallid, a mockery of what had been lost. Its weak glow lingered behind the clouds as a reminder to all of what had been rejected. They had shut out the light of God.

In addition to the natural turmoil, this fallen world was beset by a darker menace. It had been overtaken by evil and deceptive spirits. These wandered free to wreak their havoc, with no one to stand against them or cast them out. These devils and demons sought to make Terram their own, subverting natural order wherever they could. They had gained control over most of the land, leaning thousands to their influence, individuals and governments alike. Those whom they could not enslave, they attempted to destroy. They terrorized communities of survivors. Honest and moral individuals had been harassed and hunted like dogs by the sinister agents of evil. Many once decent folk were driven to the point of insanity, forced to wander the wastes in duress. The upright perished and became scarce as fine brass, while the wicked became ever more depraved.

It was a bitter mystery, why the Father had permitted darkness to prevail. In times past, He had demonstrated His sovereign grace in ways clearly seen. Again and again, he had delivered this world and its people from destruction, yet now, it seemed to most as if He had turned his back on man. Had he truly chosen thus, to depart and resign creation to the fate it had elected through rebellion? Surely, the depravity of humankind was self-inflicted.

It was they who had evoked God's enemies, the demons, with their monstrous toll. Through lies and heathen rituals, they had called them here, inviting them in. Foolish generations had opened up their homes to the evil. They had provided gateways through compromise and carelessness, as well as through certain technologies, the use and purpose of which they did not fully comprehend. These devices themselves were not wrong or blasphemous, yet they became portals and tools of evil all the same. Their misuse and abuse led to greater tragedy as some found that they could not live without them. Minds were ensnared and as a result, chaos ensued. The children turned against their parents and the earth was stricken with a curse.

Men and women were themselves changing. No one knew just how or where it began. Sometime between the beginning of the quakes and the disappearance of the sun, things like trust and love were lost to them. Something had descended in the dead of night; some malevolent sorcerer, some wicked fiend had stolen away their hearts. He had crept in and removed them, leaving behind only effigies of coldest stone. The devil's work was subtle, yet thorough. If any were not in right relation with the Father, they were robbed of their innermost heart. They could no longer hold to their spouses or care for the ones they once had loved. The searing of their consciences followed soon after. They became twisted and monstrous, in some ways more perverse than the demons themselves. For these people had once known the truth. They had heard it, yet it had meant nothing to them; nothing but a life they had thrown away. They were shadows of their former selves.

Gillean Weaver knew this subversion well, the overthrowing of one's innermost being. The cost of this was an ever-present burden to him, a sadness he must carry with him all his days. Not only had he born witness to it, he had ventured down this path himself. He had been a slave to the forces of evil, yet no more. Never again would he submit or compromise, giving in to what he knew was wrong. The forces of death had taken everything from him, and he had his loneliness to remind him of what his disobedience to the Father had cost.

His Lord had revealed the demons to him for what they were, the enemies of God and man. They were thieves, send forth to kill, steal, and destroy. Gillean only wished he had recognized their influences sooner. Perhaps then, his beloved might still be living.

She had been saved, rescued at the end, yet at terrible cost. The evil had cut short her life and had taken her away from him. The darkness had called to her so sweetly, as it had called to him for a time, enticing him to compromise and leading him further and further from the Father's light.

Gillean was thankful for what his Lord had done in securing her soul. Come to find out, He had had it in his hand all along. His beloved had rebelled, yet He had brought her back to Him and had loved her even while she cursed His name. This was an aspect of God which the temporal world did not like to acknowledge.

Gillean knew he would see his love again one day, yet why had she been taken from him? Why could not their union have been saved and restored? They had both been so innocent on the day of their wedding, made pure in heart by the Father's love. Their sacred vows, their bond had been beautiful, ordained and cherished by the one who gave them breath. His spirit had spoken thus.

There were some who had insisted that his beloved had never ascribed value to the sacred things. At times, Gillean feared this might have been true. Yet, he wished to remember her the way she had been before the darkness overtook them, the way he had viewed her that most holy day. She glided through the chapel, arrayed in white, the skin of her face and neck glowing with a wonderous brilliance. Fear was a stranger to them that day. They had held only love in their hearts.

He missed her more than mortal tongue could tell. Her absence was a burning pain, a wound unhealed in his soul. It seemed that this was something time could never mend. As long as he continued on, he would miss the embrace of the woman he loved. Losing her seemed almost comparable to losing his connection with the Father.

The very second this thought entered his mind, a sharp rebuke struck Gillean's spirit. Perhaps this was the reason she was not still with him. She had been precious to him, yet he never should have put her before his Lord. With a trembling in his bones, Gillean realized that she had been an idol to him. With tears and brokenness, he asked for forgiveness. If he had only recognized this sooner... Yet their parting may still have been unavoidable.

This world was going under. Its descent and destruction had long been foretold. All these things had occurred before. This was only the latest demise, the most recent reckoning in a sad perpetuating cycle.

Gillean knew it was unwise to question the Father, yet there were times when he found himself doing exactly that. What was the plan or purpose behind this? Was each world, each lapsing, repeating existence doomed to fail? Were all the souls lost during the cataclysms simply refuse, waisted celestial matter to be disregarded, irredeemable due to corruption and vice?

The spirit of the Father still comforted Gillean. His gentle words still answered him from time to time, even when his worries and questions seemed trivial. Hearing the still, small whisper in his mind, he was reminded that it was not given for him to know all the reasons behind their dreary plight. The important thing, his crucial calling was to trust and obey.

Despite his many failings and misdeeds, he had found favor in the eyes of the Father. He had been shown this even through his trials. The grace and provision of his Lord had never left his side. There were times when his ordeals had made it seem so, yet, deep within his heart, Gillean had known better. He had come to realize that salvation and divine love were not based on emotion; they were formed of a far lofty matter, something from far above this dusty realm which gave life to the soul.

Gillean tried to show the Father's love to others when he could, yet this was becoming increasingly difficult. In a world ruled by demons, it was hard to know who was safe. A simple act of kindness could leave you slain beside the road. All enemies were not obvious, and most were skilled in deception and illusion. They knew how to appeal to you, how to get you to lower your guard. Once you did, they would strike without mercy.

Gillean was not a violent man by nature, yet he had been forced to become a warrior. Combat was never his first choice in any situation. In recent months, it had become increasingly disagreeable to him. Yet, if he was to stay alive, he must keep fighting. The Father had commanded that he should live. To what purpose, he knew not, yet, he had received this sacred promise, that he would be protected. He had also been reassured that he would be used for good. This the Spirit had spoken. These words were secure, set in stone.

Chapter Three:
Mt. Lithmer

The old desert church seemed lifeless and vacant. Hot wind and crackling dust scoured its sides and all its once-loved dreams. Outside its boney, stone gates stood a faded sign. It read, "Mt. Lithmer." The barren yard was scattered with tombstones, markers of the long-departed dead. The congregation had fled this world. They had moved to a higher place.

Without its people, the place was confounded, gone to ruin. Loneliness possessed the now bullet-riddled walls. Gillean could feel it as he entered in. It bit into his soul. He was no stranger to it, this feeling which so easily beset him. It seemed to follow him wherever he went. There was no escaping it now that the curse had come to fruition.

This humble church had once been filled with lovely, wonderful people, the kind of people you could lend your heart to. Gentle and devout, they cared for each other as a family. They had walked in the word of God, had stood in the gap. The had abided faithfully for years, keeping the sacred trust till derision overtook them.

Everything had changed with the ordination of a new minister. Confusion had come from the wild-eyed man. He was a loud and boisterous minister with wormwood in his veins. He had shouted and slandered his way into the stand and over the all too trusting people. By his tempestuous will, all those who opposed him were trampled underfoot.

Set upon "purging the devil from their midst," he propagated strife and accusation. The madman stirred the pot until divisions had scattered the flock. The man's obnoxious familiar spirit still besieged this old building yet Gillean was not afraid. He knew he was protected by a higher name. He had come here for food and supplies and would not be frightened away until his task was complete.

Moving between the dusty pews, his boots echoed on the ancient knot-holed floor. The wood boards sagged in places, yet they remained strong enough to support weight, at least, he hoped they would. They creaked and groaned beneath his boots. The windows were still intact. Their clouded popcorn-glass panes gleamed in the faint light of midday. They quaked with the walls as distant tremors moved up from somewhere far below. These had been coming and going for several days.

The light inside grew then faded, then grew again as the clouds rushed past outside. The kitchen and dining area were Straight back past the pulpit. What he needed would be there. He side-stepped to avoid treading on a torn hymnal, yet as he did, he felt a familiar cold sensation sweep over him. He realized that he was being watched.

Continuing his careful movements, Gillean reached around his side and took hold of his slide-bolt pistol. Undoing the thin strap, he brought it up and held it ready. He stepped around the ragged altar and peered through the doorway into the dining area. It was empty, yet he did not lower his guard.

Walking over past the corner cabinets, he tapped along the wood-board floor with his boot. As clouds of choking dust billowed up, a hollow resonance rang out and he knelt to open to hidden panel long concealed.

Reaching deep within the stone-lined hole, he removed a crate of dried out victuals wrapped in thick paper. Below them, inside a sealed jar, were cans of vegetables and other dainties. These he removed as well. They had been waiting here for years and there was no guarantee that they would be eatable, yet he intended to take his chances. He would consume the food slowly, eating bits at a time until he knew it would not make him sick. Past experience had taught him this was the safest way.

From outside the thin, decaying walls, he could hear a rustling. The whistling wind could not drown out the many footfalls of those surrounding the church. Fully aware, Gillean pretended not to take notice. He gathered up what he could in a burlap sack, strapping it to his left shoulder. His departure from this place would not be simple, yet it would be. He would live. He had this sacred promise. Whatever happened, he would live.

Moving back towards the sanctuary, Gillean sensed the eerie aura of sallow candlelight. It was as he feared. His pursuers were not ragtag bandits, or even soldiers of the Assembly. The gray Mavarians had found him.

They were the stuff of legend, of myth. In former years, any who even spoke of them as being real, was credited with insanity. They were a remnant from another time, a leftover people from the world before. They had been waiting deep within the earth, biding their time until this world became weak and its people careless. They were not fully mortal, yet not entirely spirit either. It was said they were the children of unholy unions between celestial servants of God and the daughters of men. They were evil, maliciously deceptive, and above all strong. Yet they were not impervious to the weapons of man. Bullets and blades still had effect on them, as did fire.

As supposed "half-demons," they were always looking for "a master," or so he had been told. Yet Gillean believed he knew whom they served. He had seen him once, a terrible, haunting man, shadowed in some type of haughty formality. The man was called "Hector." He had tried to take away Gillean's heart once. He had temporarily succeeded in deceiving his late wife and using her to his evil and perverted ends. Gillean believed him to be the devil. Everything he had seen and everything the still, small voice had told him, seemed to point to this. He was the enemy, a monster in human from, the deceiver of the masses. It was thought that Hector was somehow in league with the Sacred Assembly, the government which ruled over this land. It had once been sworn to feed the people from the word of God, to uphold righteousness and justice. That was before. Now, they sought to cleanse the world and to subjugate all life to their twisted agenda.

      Gillean set aside his rambling thoughts as he waited before the altar. The shadows at the windows were clustering and the smell of old crusted skin wreaked around him. His ghoulish enemies tapped against the walls. They clawed at the ragged siding and tapped it with their rusty weapons. Gillean prayed. He reached out to the Father. Only He could give him the strength which was his need. Only he could preserve him and bring to pass the promise which He had given. It was moments like this which served to test his faith. He had seen enough to have been confident, yet, somehow, he always seemed to need his faith refreshed. God willed to keep him on his toes. He would not let Him become comfortable. To become so was to invite destruction.

The warped oak doors creaked and a pallid gray face pressed in. Its large, black eyes ate up the room and the sight of the man standing past the mismatched pews. As Gillean raised his gun, the creeper blinked and pulled back.

There was a chatter and buzz, then they rushed in. There were many of them. Some had found new hosts, young and agile. Others still had their ancient forms left over from centuries past: dusty, gray and calloused. Many of them had sought to pervert the image of God and man by combining their forms with those of animals. Most common was the robed body of man, crowned with the haunting head of a great owl. The enormous eyes stared damningly, yellow or black as the case may be, taunting the victim of their wrath. There was nowhere to run. They had him. Yet they did not. If his Father was for him who could stand against him?

The ghouls ran forward out flank him. Gillean prayed, his prayers reverberating in his mind. Trusting his Father to aid him, he fired. The shots went through flesh, fur, and feathers. The bodies sprawled amongst the pews. Blades and axes spun through the dry air. They clattered around Gillean as he kept shooting. He moved back quickly, not allowing himself to be trapped by the angry creatures. They kept coming, unafraid, relentless, like ants after syrup. They did not care if they were disembodied. He assumed their spirit halves would fall back to regroup beneath the earth and wait upon new words from Hector. Until God willed to bind them, they could continue to harass and torment this world. They might soon be confined in chains beneath darkness, but as of this moment, they were here, desiring his doom.

Firing through the last few rounds of the slide-bolt, he jabbed it into the back of his belt and drew out a revolver. It was one he valued. It had belonged to his late wife. He had prayed over it on the day of her untimely death. He had considered leaving it with, placing it beside her in her grave, yet he had kept it. It had served him well.

The flow of hideous people and creatures lulled and Gillean made a bolt for the back of the church. He crashed past a clutter of broken chairs and tables. He could hear the howl and chatter of the Mavarians behind him.

Ready for anything, he kicked open the backdoor and raced through. Miraculously, his path was clear. Some of the Mavarians were hobbling around the side of the church, yet they seemed slow, their movements abated by some encumbering force.

Gillean did not stop to wonder or ponder. He thanked God as he ran. He called out for speed and endurance and it was given him. In his earlier years, unhealthy drinks and foods had poisoned and oppressed his body, yet now, a leaner diet and fasting had changed him. It was as if his blood had been cleaned and he had been granted new life. The Father was with him. The croaking voices of the Marvarians would speak otherwise, yet he had learned not to listen to them. He tuned them out, keeping his face set and focused like a flint.

      The obnoxious cluck and gobble faded as he ran. God willing, the dust and winds of the desert would wipe away his trail. His pursuers possessed a hideous strength, yet they did not travel quickly over open spaces. He would lose them in the great dunes to the west and they would wonder aimlessly until they were forced to give up. Hector was not with them, and in this Gillean was relieved. He would not sleep well tonight, but he would rest. He would be thankful and would praise his God.

Chapter Three:
The Abominable Dream

Gillean tossed and turned, trapped in the confines of a feverish sleep. Sweat burned against his forehead as his dreams continued on. They were filled with a thick, all-consuming haze, yet seemed more real to him than the world from which he had drifted.

He was lost in a distant land, a dim and weary place confusing to him. The ground was composed of white, sandy soil populated with sparse growth. Saw-bladed grass and the gnarled, stunted shrubs speckled the boggy terrain. Walking with difficulty, Gillean expected any moment for the land to turn to liquid swamp. Yet it did not.

Out of the dusky gloom, loomed gargantuan structures, the likes of which he had never seen. Great ships with smokestacks rising from their decks. They lay on their sides, wrecked and rotten in the bone-dry sands. Strange craft and vehicles abounded as well; their rusty forms long forgotten in this distant reality.

All around him, haunting voices were calling. They were well known to him, yet strange: alive, yet muffled as if by the sodden shroud of death. Old friends rose from the chalk-white dust. Their eyes were a smoldering red, their faces framed by darkness. They grimy gray of their skin told him what they really were: Mavarians. But before he could successfully draw his gun, they had vanished in the mists, leaving only their echoes behind them.

 Unnerved at the sight of his long-departed brethren and sisters as the indwelt, he stumbled on, shaking and delirious from thirst. Though the fog had thickened, the air was dry, so dry that the very act of breathing cracked his lips, making them burn. In truth, it was now more like smoke. The mist held no touch of moisture or coolness at all.

 Suddenly, as he breathed it in, Gillean discovered that it was smoke. He choked on its thick, oily fumes and nearly passed out. Its stench was stifling, cutting into his lungs like rusty saws. Shielding his watery eyes, Gillean ducked low and scuttled to find clearer air. To his left, it thinned and he passed through with a fit of coughing.

 Gasping for a clean breath, he found himself on the edge of a vast field of tall, brown-gray weeds. They swayed in the windless air, bobbing seemingly of their own volition. The shadows danced with them, caught against the light of a decaying sky. It was late evening. The reddish hues in the west told him that, somehow, the sun must have returned. Yet this was not his own land, possibly not even his own world. He had traveled far, farther than he had ever been.

The thinning air was inundated with peculiar sensations. Alien vibes and curious vibrations coursed around him, like the current of some hidden electrical force, invisible, yet full of power. He sensed that life was beginning to stir all around him, perhaps hidden in the high, rusty weeds.

It was becoming difficulty to see. There was no clear path, so Gillean decided to cut across the waving field. Perhaps eventually it would have an end. Eventually, he might find some sort of landmark, something to help him gain his bearings.

As night fell in force and the air cooled, crickets began to chirp. Faint and glowing lightening bugs arose from the tangled stems. They hovered about, forming non-coherent clusters and passing on to merge with the darkness. Some seemed to spread out along the graying expanse in a ragged, diagonal line. It was as if they were showing him his appointed path.

In waking life, it might have occurred to him that trusting strange insects could prove hazardous to his health. Yet, this was a dream, and in it, his judgment was skewed.

With uneven stride, he waded through the prickly sea of weeds. The rough, tasseled leaves of the plants reached for him, clawing against his pants. It was as if they were trying to pull him back, to keep him from moving forward. Gillean shirked them off and proceeded till he saw a mass of tangled shadows rise before him.

It was a wood, tall and bristling. An autumn moon peered out of hiding above him. In its illumination, he realized the darkness had not produced a lie. The very bark of the trees was black, as black as pitch. They hung together in tight, ragged lines, like soldiers braced for a battle. Their zig-zagged limbs were covered in thorns. Some of the spines were nearly as long as his arm.

Gillean would not have ventured further, yet he had seen a light rising from beyond the wood. It glowed orange and muttered red against the black boughs, its discarded rays simmering between shadows. It was a fire, as sure as he lived. Mayhap there would be someone on the other side of the forest, some person with whom he might speak. He needed to discover where he was.

Attempting to prepare himself for the difficulty ahead, Gillean stole quietly up to the bristling brush and looked for a way through. Just ahead of him, and a little to the right, he noted a small pathway. It was no bigger than a rabbit trail, cut sloppily through the thorny growth.

Wasting little time, he took the way provided. He crept along, keeping low in the dim glow. The jutting thorns nipped and plucked at his garments. His wits were still not entirely about him, yet, he knew caution was imperative. It had saved his life before and he considered the impulse to use it a gift from God.

Nearing the other side of the prickly wood, Gillean paused and took note of what lay ahead. Through the crooked branches, he could see the flames. They rose from three massive bon-fires, ravenous, virile, consuming all that was thrown to them. About them stood an enormous throng. The people were as varied in race as they were in age. They seemed to be a cross section of all nations and creeds. They huddled close, unnaturally so, yet there was tension among them. They stood like members of a tight-knit family, bound together, yet disturbed by some agonizing, unresolved dispute. Their uneasiness alone made Gillean want to bolt.

With a new and sudden lurch of apprehension, he looked above them, past the rushing flames to the darkness beyond. His stomach dropped.

There were four of them, four hulking shapes wrapped in shadow. They were not human. With scaled, black hides and long, lanky arms they looked to have been born from the thorny trees. They towered over the reaching flames. Their teeth were curled, protruding from thin, wicked snouts. Their eyes glowed like soot-tarnished rubies, inlayed with molten glass. With one glance, he knew they could see him. They could see everything, even in the deepest shadows. Darkness was not an obstacle to them. It was their companion.

Gillean wanted to run, yet his feet were frozen. He had never felt such terror, not even the day he had lost his beloved wife.

The tyrannical lizards seemed to crackle in the ghastly glow. They stared down at the huddled crowd, and the people looked back at them, dumb and defenseless in the dark. Then the unthinkable.

Gillean watched in horror and disbelief as the people began to worship the beasts. They knelt and bowed themselves low to the earth, hailing the creatures as gods. With blabbering lips, they swore over their souls. Even the little children followed their parents and pledged their commitment. Like mindless sheep before slaughter, they offered themselves up as prey. Yet the monstrous beasts did not consume them, not physically at least.

The brutes basked in the worship, as in the turbid flames. They almost seemed to be smiling. Gillean saw the giant, bone-crushing jaws begin to move and a new wave of dread swept over him. He realized the terrible creatures were speaking.

The tongue in which they spoke was not known to him, yet the deep and mumbled words were that of a human language. They held meaning, no matter how garbled, and he knew the beasts were using their speech to intensify their hold on the minds of the captive worshipers.

This was an evil abomination. These creatures, natural or no, were never meant to be elevated above man; and no created thing was to be elevated above the creator. This was the heinous work of demons.

Without another thought, Gillean screamed out. He shouted to the people abandoning all pretense of stealth. He warned them of the evil which had entranced them, and of the dreadful penalty and judgment which would surely follow should they continue.

"Thou shall worship the Lord thy God!" He cried. "And him only shall thou serve!"

The assembled throng turned and looked at him blankly, their faces like those of timid mice, caught in the light of an open pantry door, vague and expressionless but for the slightest hints of fear. Yet the fear was not enough, or they did not comprehend. Turning back, they continued their ritual, bowing and bobbing before the hideous creatures.

The beasts themselves only smiled at Gillean. They mocked him with the blood behind their gleaming eyes. Their unheard words tore at his heart even as he prayed. His faith faltered as he realized these souls would not escape. They had chosen this fate, and their choice had been absolute.

Suddenly, his eye was caught by a twitch of movement to his left. Turning, half expecting to see another monster, he saw an old woman approaching him. She advanced on him down a subtle slope of earth. Her face was wrinkled, yet tight, as if stretched by some concealed pressure. Her visage was sour, hateful, deadly. Her eyes were dark and her teeth barred like those of a rabid dog.

By the time his mind recognized her, it was already too late. She flew towards him with inhuman speed. Strong and boney fingers clutched at his throat. He tried to fight her off, but she had strength in her, the like of which most men did not poses. As the air was choked from his wind-pipe, Gillean stared into her eyes. Though she was killing him, he met her gaze, undaunted, striking all fear from his heart. He called out to the Father, invoking the sacred name of Jesus.

Spluttering, he awoke from the dream. The wind outside was moaning and the fire in the hearth had gone out. Realizing the importance of his dream, Gillean got up and took pen to paper, writing down all he could before the details faded into obscurity.

Chapter Four:
Char'gabble

Gillean got up from the table. Laying aside his pen, he made his way over to the other side of the small dwelling. Feeding wood into the old, cast-iron stove, he went about making his preparations for morning. It was not yet light, but he felt it soon would be. The brisk, half-glow of morning always greeted him through the kitchen window, that is, if the weather permitted.

As if in response to his thoughts, the tempo of the wind increased. It beat upon the cottage in raging gusts, shaking the thin glass of the windows and battering the walls with debris. The rain fell thick, icy and poisoned upon the roof. Gillean was thankful he was not out in it. There was a scratch and shuffle at the front door, followed by a low, gravelly moan.

Gillean undid the latch and bolt, opening it just a crack. This was all the invitation Char'gabble needed. The ruffled rooster zipped inside, eyeing him with his petty and indignant gaze. Stopping to preen, he muttered his approval in a series of low, bubbling clucks. With a fiendish gleam in his yellow eyes, he leapt upon the table and shook out his feathers, dispersing tiny droplets everywhere. He crowed once, beating his wings in proud display.

He made as if to repeat the performance, yet a stern look from Gillean kept him silent. The bird had forgotten the rules of his master's house.

Sheepishly, Char'gabble hopped down and trundled off to his favorite corner. Gillean smirked as he watched his feathered friend. *You can stay inside for now, as long as you are quiet and don't play on the furniture,* he thought to himself.

He knew Char'gabble understood the rules. Though the bird was not by any means human, he was very intelligent. Gillean had not found the rooster, this rooster had found him. He had been exploring the long-abandoned ruins near the emptied city Gadd when they had met. Char'gabble had been half-starved, a pitiful and lonely creature. When he had first leapt out of the rocks, Gillean had nearly blown him away, thinking him to be a wild animal on the attack. The then scrawny rooster had clung to his leg, groaning and wailing in a voice which had seemed almost like that of a sick person. Yet, Char'gabble had not been possessed by spirits, only in need of a friend, a friend who would feed and care for him.

Gillean had allowed the clingy fowl to travel with him. Eventually, Char'gabble had permitted himself to be picked up and carried under Gillean's arm like a basket. Gillean had to be stern with him however. At first, the little rooster seemed quite the coward, whining at every unfamiliar sound. Later,

Gillean learned how to read the birds garbled mumbling and cries. He had a different sound for everything and a distinct set of vocalizations for when danger was near. Once he could recognize his warning cries, Char'gabble became the best "watchdog" Gillean had ever owned. Nothing seemed to escape his pet's attention. Many times, he was able to point out details overlooked by his master and was richly rewarded for it.

  Gillean would have taken him along to Mt. Lithmer, yet, he had deemed it unwise. Besides, for all his plucky loyalty, Char'gabble often abided by his own schedule. Occasionally, he would be waiting and ready to serve. On these days, Gillean would find him seated on his doorstep, a half-dead mouse or a twig clenched in his beak as an offering. Yet, most days he was off milling about the slopes looking for insects or some shiny trinket to add to one of his many nests. These he made in the remnants of dead thickets and in the sandy dirt behind the house. From his activities, it was apparent that he had not given up on one day finding some hens. He was determined, no matter how slim the chances. Chickens had become scarce these days, for obvious reasons. Once, Gillean had briefly considered eating Char'gabble, yet he could not bring himself to slaughter him. In the absence of human companions, this silly bird had kept him company. He knew it was unwise to become attached to an animal, yet the decision seemed to have been made for him.

As the saucy fowl nestled down for a nap, Gillean surveyed his pantry. His stores were not plentiful, yet they would suffice for the time being. He would make due until he was able to reach the nearest trading-post.

The trading-posts, the rugged, ramshackle communities bordering the deadlands were not safe. They were gathering places for criminals. They were filled with cut-throats and thieves, yet they allowed for the trading and sale of commodities on an impressive scale. For the most part, the Assembly government let them be. Unless they were looking for someone, they left them alone to their own devices, believing other concerns were more deserving of their attention. Because of this, the trading-posts were largely lawless. It was easy to be cheated, yet if one was shrewd and discreet, they might enter in with little, and leave with much-needed goods. Needless to say, he would not be bringing Char-gabble.

Gillean reached for a battered, rusted tin on the top pantry shelf. He took it down, and with great ceremony, opened it. The sweet, vigorous aroma of its contents filled his nostrils. Coffee! He only had a little left, yet he would savor its blessing while it lasted.

He scooped out a generous spoonful and dropped it into a small, dented metal strainer set atop a steel bowl. Pouring boiling water through the grounds, he breathed in as the fragrant steam ascended. Even the smell brought back the feeling of vitality.

Relishing his warm drink, he watched the rain as it swept across the glass. What had been the purpose of his dream? There was great evil in the land, and many strange, ungodly creatures roaming the wastes, yet nothing like the terrible reptiles had he ever seen. Were they truly living beings, or did they merely represent something metaphorical, some dark, spiritual oppression? Perhaps they were embodiments of the Assembly and its cruelty and perversion. But, yet, why were there four of the creatures? Why had "that woman" been there?

The sour-faced old woman was a person well known to him, a phantom from his past. Her name was Lillith and she had been the godmother of his late wife. Gillean had long believed that she had planned the downfall of their union, and had played an instrumental role in the overthrowing of his beloved's mind. Upon reflection, he was convinced that she had been in league with Hector the deceiver. Through her subtle arts and the practice of witchcraft, she had gained a foothold in the young woman's thoughts, tightening her control day by day, preparing the way for he who would complete the evil work. Although her powers had been great, Gillean had thought the evil old woman to be deceased.

Did she still live, that eldest witch whom time could not seem to cripple? Had she returned, indwelt by demons to finish some unholy design against him? This he did not know. Yet of one thing he was sure. There had been a purpose behind what he had seen. It would surely be revealed to him in due season.

Chapter Five:
The Captive Existence

Amanda could hardly feel her face. The sharp, cold had numbed it to the bone, raking its breath across her cheeks like the claws of a wild animal. Her back was a different matter entirely. Its nerves and tendons screamed as if they had been contorted into flaming knots. The pain was nearly unbearable; yet she struggled through it as she continued to work, splitting stone alongside the rest.

The rough wood of the hammer's long handle felt strangely light in her hands, yet every swing was torture. The spasms in her back and shoulders nearly crippled her. She cried out to the Father in her prayers, not knowing if they would even reach Him from this place so far removed. She had strayed from the way, and now, like so many others, she paid for her sins with agony.

They were all prisoners of this place, captives of this foreign realm. The land of Eon they called it, for existence here seemed to stretch on forever and ever. They did not feel the effects of physical aging, only the sharp, persistent pain as their bodies suffered under the grueling work.

Upon arriving here, her surroundings had appeared quite different than they now were. This world had been lush and fragrant, entirely appealing to her senses. It had been soft, green and brimming with life and vibrance. The abundant fruits and vegetables had been sweet to the taste, replenishing and satisfying. Too late, Amanda had learned that these had been enchanted or drugged with some evil, binding toxin, or some combination of the two which prevented her escape.

Whenever anyone attempted to wander or flee their designated area, the effects of the poison became painfully apparent. They would begin as a slow tick and would progress to spasms and a rising temperature which wracked the body, throwing it into febrile seizures and convulsions. Eventually, you would succumb to it and pass out into a numbing blackness. Upon reawaking, you would find yourself back where you had started, at the cursed quarry with a hammer in your hand and a full day's work ahead of you.

The fruit was now bitter, tasting of sulfur and stale potash. They ate as a matter of survival, loathing it even as they chewed. The trees and hedges were faded, as if artificial. The darkness of their clustered depths was full of eyes, spiteful and sadistic. The woods were inhabited by evil, wicked spirits which fed off every harmful emotion, perpetuating them tenfold. Their presence was always abiding, watching, feeding off those trapped here. No one was ever fully alone here, and none had peace within.

Amanda had not been the first misguided soul to become imprisoned in this world. She had realized that others were present a short time after her arrival, yet by then she had eaten of the cursed fruit and it was too late to flee. She had been warned by a stranger. By God's grace, all who came to that place were warned. Yet, believing she knew better, she had not heeded the sage advice.

Through her kind heart and compassionate nature, Amanda had made friends here. In their resting hours, she did her best to encourage and comfort the depressed and despairing. More than once, she had actively intervened in preventing suicides. Though she had never known the kindness of a mother, she had a mother's heart. This was something which this place could never take away from her.

Since her imprisonment in this alien world, she had noticed changes in her physical appearance. At first, they were alarming, yet she slowly learned to live with them. Her face and arms seemed to have thinned and her stature had increased by at least a foot. The former, she thought, could be attributed to a loss of weight, yet she could not account for the latter. Her hair had lightened, becoming soft and fine. It still tangled as was its habit, yet not as often. It had grown long, almost to her waist. In order to work, she kept it bound up behind her head. It pulled at her scalp and was sometimes uncomfortable, yet even so, she had no desire to cut it. In some strange way, it was a solace to her, a pleasant blessing, one last goodly gift from God.

She had never considered herself vain, or even beautiful, yet she had come to value herself, understanding that she was fearfully and wonderfully made. The Father had created her thus. He had spoken thus, and there was no lie in Him. She knew the same held true for the other prisoners, both women and men, and through the reading of the sacred Word, she attempted to show them so. She remembered her husband, the one she had lost, the one she had betrayed. He had told her she was beautiful. Every day of their shared life, he had told her. He had believed it, and his value of her had warmed the deepest parts of her heart. Remorse and regret still haunted her, yet she was comforted with the sure knowledge that he had gone to be with the Father.

The fact that Amanda had the Word of the Father was a miracle in and of itself. She had found it in the dark and dreadful forest. She had been wandering, testing the limits of her confinement. Her head had just begun to split with the aura of mounting pain, when she stumbled upon the ancient, leather-bound tome resting sheltered beneath a cluster of ferns. Upon realizing what it was, Amanda snatched it up. She had clutched it to her breast, and had ran with it to her tiny hovel. There, she kept it safe, preserving it for the good of all who needed it. The overseers seemed unaware of its existence. They seemed to turn a blind eye to the words passed between the faithful and the gathering around her dwelling. All the same, she took precautions. The Father's Word was too precious a treasure to risk losing.

    Amanda immersed herself in those aged pages every chance she got. Though escape seemed impossible at the present, she believed in her heart that a way would be made. When it was provided, she knew that somehow the Word of the Father would prove essential. It would surely be the key.

Chapter Six:
Loneliness

Gillean was beset by loneliness. He still spoke to the Father and occasionally voiced his thoughts to Char'gabble, yet it wasn't the same. He missed conversing with other mortal humans. He longed for companionship and friendly banter, the tokens and occurrences of his former existence.

Understanding the love of the Father and His continued watch-care over him, he knew he was never alone, yet he felt for all the world that he was. His continuing isolation was slowly killing him. The sadness of his plight would consume him if he let it, if he did not find ways to occupy his mind. It seemed to drift in through the walls of the cottage and seep deep into his bones. He could not shut it out no matter how he tried.

He missed his beloved wife and how they had been in those distant days of old. Those golden, joyous days when her heart was tender. They had known love then, real love, closeness and warmth, the likes of which now lived only in the occasional dream. Those moments spent with her would live forever, seared into his soul. Gillean thanked God for them. He was grateful for the marvelous treasure he had been granted. He had been a part of something holy, to know and comprehend the depth of sacred union with a soul and flesh pleased to join unto his own. They had been bound together within a three-fold cord, a reflection of the holy Trinity, a symbol of the one, true heart of God.

Now, with all this behind him, Gillean struggled each and every day just to fight off despair. He had known his share of friends, comrades, and acquaintances, yet none had lasted. One by one, they had perished or been drawn away. Some might still be alive. They might have lived on, surviving out there somewhere in the endless expanse of this fading world. If he searched long enough, desperately enough, he might even find a few of them. Yet, no matter the strength of his resolve or efforts, he would never again regain what had been ripped from his arms, the treasured beauty of his first love. She was a distant haunting dream, safe in the Father's arms, yet never again to rest in his.

Countless times, he had questioned God, though he well knew it might be a sin. He had shouted to the heavens in nights of anguish, ignorant of all but his grief. He knew he was selfish, yet somehow it did not seem to matter much anymore. Everyone else had departed. He recalled that, long ago, a pastor had spoken of "dying to self." He had attempted that before, when he was married. He had given all he could, sacrificing until the point of exhaustion, yet it had been to no avail in the end. Still it was something he wished to accomplish, in spite of the fact that he was alone, perhaps for nothing more than the justice of denying himself. He had fasted many a time. In fact, this was when his most vivid dreams occurred, such as the one he had most recently had. He devoted hours to the study of the Father's Word, attempting to learn how he might better himself and grow in his relationship with Him. He prayed without ceasing, crying out for those he had never met. He wanted to help them somehow, yet, he knew not where they were, or even how to find them. Death waited all about him, simply waiting for one misstep to swallow him up.

Suddenly Gillean realized what was wrong. An ancient scripture passed through his mind and lingered before the innermost parts of his soul. *And though I bestow all my goods to feed the poor, and though I give my body to be burned, and have not charity, it profiteth me nothing.*

All those years behind him, he had struggled to keep his heart alive, yet in his complacency, it had hardened in a way he had not realized. He realized the toll this brutal world was taking on one of God's greatest and most precious gifts. He needed love, not just for himself, but for humanity. He needed a wider love, an empathy to shatter complacency. He needed a wider, more abounding, life-filled, light-filled love from above; an unconditional one for those around him, even the murderers and the criminals. He needed a love like the Father.

He would ask for this, and with prayers and tears, he would seek it out. He felt sure that God would grant it to him. In this realm of abounding evil, it was more than needful, it was essential. Nothing would be healed without it.

Chapter Seven:
The Message

In a distant realm, far removed from sight and mortal thought, there was much unrest. Lightening crackled out across the blackened sky. The jagged lines burst neon white and purple in the folds of towering storm. These brilliant bursts flared and faded, only to return and double. The lightening was dry, burning the heavy air, rebuking the winds. It struck again and again. It lashed and spread until it covered the sky above the valley like the beating wings of some enormous electric firebird.

From a high and rocky hill, a stranger watched the storm. He was tall and thin, surrounded by shadows. They clung to him, almost causing him to vanish in the night. Though he was old, older than the hills, his face possessed a youthful glow. He was not ugly or misshapen in any way, yet his features coalesced unnaturally, almost as if they were fake.

The tall man wore a suit, a fine one, tailored uniquely for him. It was black, the color of moonless midnight. The long hem of his jacket billowed out behind him in the blustering tempest. It fluttered as he lifted his arms, hands outstretched as if to seize the wind.

Standing there, overlooking that hidden valley, he conducted the storm. With wide, exalted and exaggerated gestures, the man did his work. His dark and blasphemous powers besieged the skies. He could not fully master creation, for he was not the creator, in fact, he was at enmity with the same. Yet, there was evil in the lightening, and this fed his efforts, bending its kinetic current to his will.

Concentrating the flaring bolts, the tall man swung his arms around, gathering momentum. He reeled as if drunken on the power, a maniac in the midst of madness. With sudden exultation, he struck the air with his clenched fists.

An explosion of pale, electric light lit his skeleton smile. The air reverberated with a boom. The purple rend stabbed repeatedly, waking the earth and burning the trees. They danced as pillars of flame, caught in the furry of unholy wrath. The time had come for the loosing of evil, a sea change in the world of warning spirits.

Far below, the hidden valley smoked and sizzled. No longer concealed by shrubbery, a sallow-white mausoleum stood, silhouetted against the putrid flame. There was a long, dark crack in its side. The fissure was little more than a foot at its widest point, yet it had been sufficient. Those confined there had been released. Their master had work for them to accomplish.

With a ragged gasp, Amanda sat up in bed. Outside, the storm raged on, yet it was not the lightening which had woken her. She listened again, now fully awake, willing whatever it was to repeat itself. She waited, holding her breath in the dark. Still, nothing.

Getting up, she reached for a candle and the precious Word of the Father. She stayed up, reading for some time until the blessed scriptures calmed her. She held and pondered the words in her heart. She treasured them, as always, yet Amanda felt there was something more she must do.
Taking up an ancient fountain pen, she dipped it in the inkwell and set the pointed tip to paper.

The paper was precious, a finite resource, valuable beyond measure. She needed to use it wisely. Her words must be just right. They must be concise, best set to fit the meaning of their purpose. She told of her dream and of the tall man in the dark suit. She knew his name. She had known it for quite some time. He was Hector the deceiver. It was he who had led her to betray her late husband and had imprisoned her in the folly of her youth.

Finally, she wrote of herself. Amanda related her plight and the sorrows of her heart. She knew not why she did this, only that the urge told her it was imperative. She doubted anyone would ever read it. If they did, they might well consider her insane. Amanda did not care. What had she left to lose?

Placing her pen back beside the grimy inkwell, she held the crinkled sheet of paper in trembling hands. Slowly she folded it and placed it in the Word for safe keeping. Unbeknownst to her, it would be kept, yet it would also be shared. This was its determined purpose. This was the will of the Father.

Chapter Eight:

Rescue form Wolves

The snarling of the great wolves was terror to the soul. They were ravenous, long starved to suit the evil designs of their mistress. She wished them well-motivated for the hunt.

Eelya Price was a relatively small woman. Her short, red hair and porcelain face gave her a pleasant, almost desirable impression. Yet there was nothing desirable left in her soul. What she lacked in stature, she made up for in sheer meanness. Despite her tender appearance, her heart was cruel, as bitter and cold as frost upon a stony step. She was a sadist through and through.

Born to poor share-cropping parents, she had risen through her cruelty and deception to become the mistress of her own lands. All her slaves and servants feared her, for with her, death was never far off. She was a harlot and a murderer. She was as bold as any man and twice as strong. It was her familiar spirits which gave her strength. She had invited them in, had welcomed them in lieu of a God she would not accept. Eelya believed that she had power over them and they were subservient to her whims. It was they who had allowed her to believe thus. They played along like a wounded wild ape that is taken in by a loving family. The creature will feign subservience and acceptance of them as its masters, all the while growing and becoming stronger, sharpening its teeth in the dark of night. When its strengthening is come to fruition, and the trust gained is solid and complete, it shall strike. The beast shall leap upon them in an hour they do not expect, slaying them in their ignorance. So, it was with Eelya and her demons. They were only biding time. Yet while they waited, she was becoming more and more like them.

She sat in the shade of her veranda, listening to the sounds of the raging wolves. They were overeager for the hunt. They could taste blood in the air, potent and unstilled, flowing free in the veins of a fugitive.

One of her slaves had escaped. The man was not much use to her, but an example must be made. This was the way of things.

She hated him. He had considered himself pious, this was evident. He had tried to corrupt the others with his vain pretense of religion. Every time she looked at him, she could sense a disquieting quality. It was as if he believed himself above her. This she had not been willing to tolerate. She had ordered him flogged, and he had been, again and again, yet it had not broken him. There were other scars already covering his back. That same sad brightness still glowed in his eyes, infuriating her soul. His flight had not been altogether unforeseen.

He would not get far, just far enough to tire himself out. Her wolves would run him down, and he would serve as their supper.

As she heard the rusty cages opened, she laughed. She sprang up and demanded that her horse be saddled. She would ride out behind her precious pets, allowing them to run ahead, catching up later to savor the carnage they wrought. The spectacle would surely be gruesome and she was enamored with the thought. Justice would be sweet.

It took Eelya nearly a full hour to catch up. Riding out across the plain, she approached the sloping foothills to the south. Nearing a dead and dried out wood, she listened hard for the snarls of her pack. The winds were absent and she could note their scattered tracks traced between bits of brush and scrub. It would not be much longer now. There was only so far a man could run.

At a dusty gap between the white and leaning trees, Eelya's horse slowed to a trot. Suddenly, she caught sight of them, her precious wolves. They were lying sprawled and lifeless amongst the bleached trunks. She gave out a wail as she realized they were dead. What had happened? Anger began to boil in her blood as a darker hue suffused her cheeks. There had been no shots fired and no man could have slain them barehanded. These were more than flesh and fur.

Galloping up to the scene of slaughter. She caught sight of one lone wolf still living. He was the alpha of the pack and by far the strongest of them all. The fur on his neck and back bristled like spines as he faced his quarry. The filthy slave was trapped, his back braced against a massive, lifeless oak. His eyes were wide, yet they held no fear, instead they radiated a firm, unyielding resolve. Without a twitch of tremor, the man stared down the beast. He was unarmed, yet not defenseless. Eelya could feel it. She detected something far more formidable than the teeth of her prized wolf. The knowledge of this only served to increase her rage. This ought not to be. Surely, the Father had abandoned this man, had left him here to the whims of her merciless will. Why the blazes was he being protected.

As the ragged fugitive continued to stare, the wolf gave a whimpering whine. Wobbling backwards, the beast fell, vomiting out its last breath. The great wolf lay silent in the dust, no more to devastate or consume.

Eelya screamed. She charged forward in her fury, the horse foaming at its mouth. There would be no escape for him, this one who dared defy and insult her authority, who had killed her cherished beasts by the power of his God. She would make him pay. After she had crippled and disabled him, she would allow her sadistic nature to take control.

She would become, fully and truly, the monster her demons had made her.

Just then, there was a gust of wind from the eastern desert. The lifeless trees shivered and shook, their rattling boughs witness to something beyond her sight. The horse sensed it, too, and stumbled to an abrupt stop. It stood there as if dumbfounded, stricken by some unheard command.

As the weary man persisted in his defiant stare, the woman's hatred of him increased by leaps and bounds. Reaching behind her, she drew out a short-barreled repeating rifle from its holster. Its cast coating beamed a dull silver in the faint light. She took aim at his gut, wishing only to wound. Her knife would do the rest. Her finger touched the trigger, yet she never took the shot.

A percussive blast ripped through the splintered boughs and slammed into her shoulder. Eelya fell, the wind knocked from her lungs. She did not even have time to scream out before hitting the ground. The horse leapt and pranced aside, leaving her exposed to the unseen enemy. She knew she was as good as dead.

The slave, whose name was Mathias, watched his tormentor fall. He had believed the Father's promise that he would be delivered, yet he was still amazed. With some small amount of shame, he realized he had not fully comprehended the truth in his heart. Stepping away from the pale oak tree, he looked to the edge of the wood from whence his rescuer approached.

The man was large, yet lanky. His arms were thick and muscular and he carried himself as one accustomed to battle. He wore the shirt and coat of a hermit, a wide-brimmed hat atop his head. His boots were those of a soldier, perhaps of the Assembly, yet he did not seem like one of them. Being well armed, he held a slide-bolt pistol in his right hand, and the strap of a large pack in his left. A dingy revolver was tucked in his belt and a leaf-shaped blade hung at his side.

Initial reaction to this man was one of fear and hesitation, yet, as he drew nearer, he felt a calm pass over him. This was a child of the Father, like himself. Somehow, he knew this. The fact was sure, secured in his spirit. He would be able to trust him.

"Greetings, sir," said Gillean, walking up to him as if out of a dream.

"Better now. I seem to have been protected. The Father was with me...forgive me, no, I was with Him. He granted me grace and spared me."

"I see," Gillean agreed, looking around at the slain wolves. "That He did."

"I'm just sorry the woman was wounded. She is not herself, not really. She is oppressed by darkness."

"It was needful. Besides, she is not dead. She may live still. It is for the Father to decide."

They both looked over at Eelya. She was breathing still, bleeding yet unconscious. Gillean found it difficult to pity her, yet he determined he would bind up her wound.

He walked over and removed the knife from her belt, checking for other weapons as well. After doing this, he inspected the shoulder. The bullet had passed straight through, shattering her scapula. Depending on the extent of nerve damage, she would most likely never have use of that arm again.

Eelya remained unresponsive as Gillean tended to her. When the dressing had been firmly secured. He rose and turned his attention to the horse. It had been standing nearby, waiting patiently for its fallen mistress. Taking its bridle, he secured his pack behind the saddle and made sure the girth and cinch were secure.

"I'm headed west," Gillean said. "Going to a trading-post up that way. You're welcome to accompany me if you wish. The horse is strong, he can carry two."

"What about her?" Mathias questioned, looking back at the pale woman.

"We leave her." Gillean answered firmly. "She won't let go her spirits and we don't need them encumbering us. She has her reward."

Mathias wanted to object, but he did not. He knew that the big man had spoken true. The woman's fate was not their concern. She would live or die, depending upon her own choice and the will of the Father.

Gillean mounted first, followed by Mathias who climbed up behind him with some little difficulty, confessing he had never ridden a horse before. Saying a brief prayer for the woman lying in the dust, they departed, riding west, leaving the faded forest behind them. Gillean could tell their newly acquired mare was weary. He let her trot at her own pace. They would stop to make camp before long, after they had put some distance between them and this place. There was no telling what other sinister entities might be lurking nearby. This had never been a safe region, even before the old world had fallen.

"Are you a holy man, a pastor?" Gillean asked, keeping his gaze on the horizon.

"In a way, I suppose I am."

"You suppose?"

"I believe I've been called by God as a pastor, yet I was never ordained. The Church never saw fit to do so."

"well, I can tell you God is greater than any church, or any other organization subverted by man. It's the Father's calling that counts. If He says you are a pastor then you are a pastor. Men can get in the way if they wish, yet woe betide those who do. In my experience, it's unwise to stand between the Father and his sovereign will. You had the look of a holy man back there. Something in your eyes. That's why I asked. Not many men could stand like you did, facing those creatures calmly like you did."

"My strength comes from God. Apart from him, I can do nothing."

"Your faith does you credit. You are a true pastor as far as I'm concerned, more worthy of the title than others I have known."

With this, the two travelers introduced themselves, Mathias taking the initiative. Gillean did not give out his true name readily or often, yet he did now. He felt he could trust the man with which he rode.

In past years, he had been a fugitive of the Assembly. They had hunted him for crimes of "treason" and "sedition," imprisoning him twice in their wretched camps. Despite his wish to never face that fate again, he was not as concerned as he had been in years past. Most of those seeking his capture or destruction had themselves departed from this life.

Since the first, great and devastating war which had poisoned the earth, the population of Terram had been dwindling. It had been further affected by the toll of the recent war of resistance against the Assembly. The bloody rebellion had been an attempt led by the rebels, known as the Sons of Veritas, to liberate the common people from the yoke of oppression. They had failed in the end. Despite their resources, the ruthless tactics of the enemy had proven too much for them. The Assembly government had gained the final victory, yet at devastating cost. They had lost tens of thousands, perhaps millions, and had succeeded in destroying most of the modern cities in the process. Their forces still stood watch, a hungry bear stalking all those who would live on, but they were wounded and weakened. Their establishment was a fraction of its former strength, a ghost of what it had been. All the same, it was best to avoid them when possible. The most dangerous and brutal regimes were those with nothing left to lose.

In the dusty light of evening, Eelya stirred. It was the agony which had forced her back to consciousness. It gouged and screamed from her shattered shoulder, like a busted hive of white-hot killer bees. She could not move her arm. Turning over, she gasped and gnashed her teeth, cursing her misfortune and every living soul. It was then she realized she was not alone.

One of the fallen wolves, one she had believed to be deceased, was struggling it its feet. It raised its scruffy, matted head and looked at her, not with loyalty, but with hunger. In those glassy black eyes, there was nothing but death. The beast would dine tonight after all.

Chapter Nine:
Discovery

The darkness was closing in on them when they finally stopped. They made camp for the night in a sunken, sandy bottom below a curved, misshapen hillside. The location was well suited to their need as it would allow them to construct a fire without the flames being easily visible from a distance. The glow would be partially reflected against the backdrop of the hill yet would be reduced by its numerous rocky folds.

There was plenty of aged wood around, most of it poking out of the crusted earth at odd angles and lining the slopes of the hills. There was even an old, petrified log, to which Gillean had secured the horse's reigns. He felt bad that they had not much food for the poor creature. They would share with her what they had, and perhaps find more suitable feed once they reached the trading post. They might end up selling or exchanging the horse. He would talk it over with his companion.

It had long been a strict law of the Assembly that horses were never to be ridden. Gillean believe it stemmed from some moronic view passed on by the High Bishops, that horses were a symbol of the Lord's triumphant return, and therefore to be treated as sacred. They had made them off limits to common men and women, keeping those that remained in special reserved parks, and sanctuaries. Some fringe rebel groups still used them, and of course, outlaws.

Gillean cared not for the laws and statues of that tyrannical government, yet, the animal would almost certainly draw unneeded attention. Many of the wasteland and desert folk were superstitious concerning such things, and might give them trouble. All things considered, it would probably best for all, the horse included, to turn her loose and let her find her own way back.

Settling in beside the blazing fire, the outlaw and the pastor ate a light supper. After they had finished their repast, Gillean took out his most prized possession, the sacred Word of the Father, bound in black leather. He began to read and Mathias read along with him, becoming engrossed in the truth of the divinely inspired text. They discussed its deeper meanings, its age-tested wisdoms and its powers of enlightenment.

It was good to speak and dwell upon such things. Gillean had surely missed conversations such as these. He had longed for them in his soul throughout the faded, lonely years. It had been nearly an eternity since he had experienced fellowship such as this, perhaps not since his time with the Sons of Veritas.

The hour was growing late. Mathias had finally drifted off to sleep, exhausted from the day's harrowing events. Gillean told himself he would soon be doing the same. He knew he needed the rest, yet something inside compelled him to keep reading.

Searching for a scripture he could not quite remember, he thumbed through the ragged pages of the Word. Suddenly, a dingy scrap of oddly colored paper fell out onto his pantleg. It was old, older than any paper he possessed. It did not belong to him, yet, what was it doing in his book? The paper was covered in scrawled writing, smudged and smeared, yet still barely legible. Holding it up to the firelight for examination, he began to read.

At first, the words shocked him. He did not know what to think of them. The message spoke of the tall man, Hector the deceiver, the one who had seduced and influenced his late wife to follow a path depravity and destruction. The words told of a happening, a dream or vision in which the man had summoned an unholy lightening-storm. He had used it to scorch a valley and break an opening in some sort of tomb, releasing some mystic force of evil.

To anyone else, all this would have seemed preposterous. It would have sounded delusional, the ravings of some deranged lunatic driven mad by the curses of the dead-lands or the burn of endless desert. Yet, Gillean was well aware of the dark man.

He had encountered him before, and knew of his devilish crafts. Simply knowing that he was still at his malevolent work kindled a flame in Gillean's bones. He knew that vengeance belonged to his Lord, yet he could not help the way he felt. He longed to see some kind of retribution upon the evil one, the dark man who had stolen away his first love, the bride of his youth. He did not know if Hector was impervious to blades and bullets. Part of him believed that he was not, yet, just as strong a conviction told him that he might be. Gillean had once seen an angel threaten him with a sword. Hector had himself thrown a knife at the adversary and had fled away. If he could somehow harm, or even destroy that appalling son of perdition, he just knew it would bring him satisfaction.

Yet, even as he thought these things, Gillean was convicted. The still, small voice rebuked his vengeful ruminations as only it could. The correction was with charity, but also solemn sternness. He knew better than to disregard these warnings. That was a road he had ventured down before, and he had payed dearly for his mistake.

Struggling to reclaim his focus, Gillean read on. The letter, for this was what it had become, told of a captive in a far-off place, a young woman held in Hector's grasp. She was with others, all unfortunate souls who had been lured into a trap. They were imprisoned and forced to work under enchantment. They had little hope of escape. Still, the young woman seemed determined to devoutly trust in the Father. Her heart and soul seemed embodied in her writing, and she appeared clearly to him, as clearly as if she stood in the fire before him.

Gillean was deeply conflicted. He wanted to believe in this woman and her moving words. He wanted to trust that the letter was legitimate and sincere, a cry for help delivered to him by way of the Father through the Word. Yet, doubt and skeptical thoughts overwhelmed his mind. How could any of this possibly be reality? He had heard of nothing like it ever before. Surely, this was some type of profane witchcraft. A cunning trick of Hector himself. How could he trust a scrap of paper, the true origins of which he did not know?

He tucked the half crumpled note back into the pages of the word. He would have to pray concerning it, sleep on it until his mind was clearer. Maybe, the Father would give him discernment. Even if he did, what would he, what could he do? He would require direction as well.

Placing the Word of the Father securely in his pack, Gillean lay down, his head beside the glowing flames. The warmth of the daytime had long since fled and the ground was cold, devoid of comfort. Still, he did not have to wait long for sleep.

Gillean was walking through a dark room. All about him, he could feel the pulse and vibration of the air, as if it was being drawn by some immense set of lungs. As he crossed a thin and polished threshold, the walls grew lighter, brighter as if infused with a living energy. On tides of golden, leaf-strewn wind he was propelled forward. The room was now a forest clearing. The trees were alive, springing up in every type and variety, their green, glowing leaves moist with morning dew.

In the center of the softly-lit glade, stood the woman, Amanda. He knew it was her just as surely has he breathed. She glowed with a vibrance that could only come from the spirit of the Father. She was covered in cuts and scrapes, yet she was beautiful, more beautiful than any woman he had ever seen. Her eyes stared into his and made him feels small, fearful of what she might think of him, of his unbelief. Why had her message been sent to him? Had it been God.

Ever so slightly, she moved towards him, her eyes full of soft light, yet strong and searching wonder. Though he knew his heart was behaving foolishly, he found himself wanting to be with her, to know her spirit and soul. He found himself attracted to her in almost every way, he could not deny it. Her presence awoke something inside of him, something higher than his thoughts or powers of reason. It made him want to be better, holier, the way he was meant to be for the glory of the Father. In that moment, Gillean knew, he had to find her.

    Waking up early before dawn, while Mathias still slept beneath his cloak, Gillean rummaged through his pack. Taking out pen and paper, he began to write. It was almost fully light when he finished. With careful hands, he slipped the letter between the pages of the Father's Word and rose up to tend the fire. Soon, they would have to be moving on.

Chapter Ten:
Dry Bones

The land was changing. It was becoming rugged, torn and broken by jutting pinnacles of rock. These lunged and twisted their way into the arid sky, rising from the cracked earth like long-forgotten rib cages. Their pathway wound between them, occasionally swinging wide to avoid a chunk of fallen stone. It was said that this place was once inhabited by an ancient tribe. Gillean wondered how anyone could exist in such a place. There was no water to speak of, on the surface at least. If it lay beneath, it must have been fathoms and fathoms below them. A person could dig until their arms broke before they reached any amount of life-sustaining moisture.

Up head, the Spiderback hills began their uneven slope. Littered with remnants of privet and briar, they stood unyielding against the warming winds. Their triangular points angled out and to the east. The bare stones became black and sooty gray, streaked with rusty iron and the leavings of volcanic spew. Shale and pumice clattered loose, disturbed by some small rock dweller, a coney or pika. The atmosphere was still, sleepless with a touch of sorrow. Both Mathias and Gillean could feel it. It was a hard feeling to explain. The aura hung like a cloud and grew stronger as they progressed higher. It was as if the rocks themselves had been weeping, pierced and permeated by some deep-set sorrow.

Mathias's countenance fell. He breathed in and a distant look passed over his eyes. Gillean could tell that man sensed something deeper, more profound.

"Something terrible happened here," he said. "The Spirit of the Father grieves in this place."

"I feel it too. Do you think we should turn around? Are you sensing a warning?"

"No, just sadness. Overwhelming sadness."

So, they went on, headed steadily upward as the dark rocks closed in around. The sound of the mare's hooves echoed in the stillness. The sky, which had been clear, was now beset with ghostly clouds. They felt alone in this haunting place, cut off from all else that lived.

It was not long before they came across a ravine. The narrow gorge stretched out between the curved peaks, cut out of the rock as if by some giant hand. Its sides and edge were lined with thick, maroon briars, yet they could see clearly into its depths. It was filled with bones, the bones of children. Half crushed skeletons lay piled atop each other and strewn against the ragged sides. There must have been thousands of them, all discarded here, thrown away like rubbish. This was the reason for the sadness, the cause of the Spirit's grieving.

They stopped and looked upon this scene of death, this mass grave forgotten in the hills. Who were they and what had befallen them? This was a desolate place, so far from hearth and home.

"The lost children," Gillean breathed. "So, this was their fate."

"The lost children?"

"Yes. Just before the last rebellion, the government abducted mass amounts of children from across the land. They said they were going to educate them, train them up so they could survive. I guess these were the ones who didn't make the cut."

"You mean they..."

"That's right. Mass execution has always been their forte. Their philosophy is, if you can't redeem or cure it, you kill it. Such lovely people. God shall surely judge them."

"But if they didn't make the cut, why slaughter them? Why go through the trouble? Why not give them back to their parents?"

"I suppose they thought that would be like admitting defeat. You can bet they justified it. They always do. Besides, those children had seen too much. Rumor was that all the abducted were taken to Arius, the secret and forbidden city. That's where the governing assembly meets. There's no coming back from there, not unless you've sold your soul. You know that, Mathias."

Mathias nodded, still dumbfounded by the horrible sight. He had long witnessed the brutality of this fallen world, yet he still endeavored to see the good in it wherever he was able. He did not believe as some did, that God had given up on man.

"Do you believe the Father took them in His arms, their souls I mean?" He asked, turning away.

"Yes pastor, I truly do. I've known the Father for quite a while. He's never changed and there is no shadow of turning with Him. He's never left a child out in the cold, or condemned one as lost, no matter what men may say. They are precious in His sight, every single one. Their names are all written in His book and He won't ever let them go. It's a fearful thing to slay one of his children, Mathias. I pity the souls of whoever was responsible. The Father shall not hold them guiltless."

Thinking back, remembering from the deepest corners of his mind, Gillean recalled a story. It was a story of a miracle, a resurrection unto life. There had been a man, a prophet of God who had come across a place very similar to this one, a valley of dead bones. The bones had been dry, lying lifeless for a great period of time. Gillean had believed that those to whom the bones belonged had been forgotten or unwanted, seeing as none had come to bury them.

God had spoken to the prophet, asking him if these bones could live as once they had. The prophet had answered Him, stating that God would surely know. The Lord had then answered him with a command, telling him to prophecy over the bones, that they might hear His word. He had said He would cause life and breath to enter in to them and flesh and skin to cover them. In truth, He vowed he would give the slain men back their life, if the prophet would only speak the words given him. Of course, he did, and the Father had performed the miracle, raising up those long-forgotten souls for His glory.

In this desolate sadness, Gillean could not hope that the Father might do the same again. He said a prayer in faith and waited with bated breath. Yet, as he feared, nothing happened. The bones remained dead, cold, and forgotten, trapped in this lonesome place. There would be no miracle today.

Softly, Gillean heard the still, small voice. His heart was moved as it was touched by the words. It was all he could do to hold back the tears. The voice was laden with sadness, yet there was a joyful hope intermixed with its tone.

It is not right that they return to this world. They are happy where they be. They do not wish to depart the light. Do not mourn them. Mourn their loss to this world and for the great sin which has separated them from their parents. These are they which would have stemmed the tide, the gifts of God which were sent to heal this land. The gifts have been rejected, yet they live as I live. These were called unworthy, yet they were not so. This world was not worthy of them.

Chapter Eleven:
The Hindrance

Amanda was chilled to the bone. The rain had been falling since early morning, drizzling down in gusting torrents. They had not been allowed a reprieve from their arduous tasks, not until the storm had grown too wild to withstand. By then, the overseers had had their fill of the weather. They had disbanded their stations, leaving the captives to own devices. It many have simply been her imagined perception, yet it seemed as if they were beginning to care less and less about their duties. She had observed their brutality against those who fell out of line, and their harsh eagerness to press the prisoners into the start of each day. Yet, they did not watch them as closely as they once had. The hours of labor had been growing shorter. The guards seemed to anticipate "quitting time," as if they had something else to do, some other errand requiring their attention. She also noted that the guards were never around after they were dismissed, leaving the enchantments of the place to keep the captives contained. The dark man, Hector, had not been around either. In fact, it had been some time since she, or anyone had seen him. This seemed like a positive thing, yet somehow, it caused a foreboding. Either the devil was on hiatus or he was busy: busy accomplishing evil.

Some of the others wished to speak with her, but she could not. There was no thought in her mind, but to recover from the cursed damp and cold. One or two of the men wished to follow her, desirous of her company. She ignored them at first. She hoped they would understand her silence as it was intended. She had never had to defend herself here, yet she believed she could if it came to that. Amanda had become strong through her struggles. Though she was worn and weary, she would find the strength to knock out an attacker. Though she seemed slim and pale, her pain and desperation were forces to be reckoned with.

They finally took the hint, breaking off pursuit and heading off to seek the company of others. Amanda pulled her shawl tight, yet kept her head held high. She did not want to draw attention to herself, yet she knew she must appear confident. For the first time since she had discovered the truth of this place, she felt hunted, stalked by something unseen. There was something hidden in the gray, green trees, some sneering evil eyeing her beyond those threaded boughs. What did it want? She had to be strong. She was almost to her hovel. Even now, she could see its mud-brown shape, dark and huddled against the wood.

With the rushing rain still lashing at her, she ran for the door. It opened at her touch and she fell inside; the spattering drops skipped and leapt as if to follow her. Coughing, she blundered around, shaking and shivering as much as she ever had. It was not long until she found a candle and matches tucked away out of moisture's reach. She lit it and set it on the table by her bed. It cast a hovering glow over the room as she changed, attempting to rub her skin dry in the process. She had to make a fire.

Amanda was thankful she had stashed some logs and kindling in her wood box beside the hearth. Others who had not been so thoughtful might have to do without. The flue was dripping, yet she had dry tinder. She set about arranging the wood and lighting the wads of pine straw at its base. Thankfully, she had a pleasant blaze in no time, and the room was successfully warmed.

Though the fire burned hot and bright, it took Amanda longer to shake the cold from her bones. She stayed near it, sitting on the floor, rocking back and forth and trying not to think of her life before this place. This was harder than she wanted to admit. Every day, she struggled to shut out regret just as much as she slaved to fight through the days of backbreaking work.

A few minutes more, and she began to absorb some of the warmth. She scooted away from the charred hearth and pulled herself up. She coughed again and let forth an explosive sneeze. Amanda knew she was getting sick, yet there was little she could do about it, other than seizing the opportunity for more rest. She did not know if there was feverfew in this world, the one of the typical remedies of her childhood. She had not seen any. She would have to search for some later if she could. Amanda did not know what befell those who became deathly ill. If she became too sick and weak to work, what would the overseers do? Would she be granted leniency or would she be punished, perhaps slain as one considered worthless. She decided not to think on this further.

Stepping dizzily over to her bed, she sat down and reached to the shelf above it. With another, half-stifled cough she removed the Father's Word from its hiding place and opened it. She began to read where the pages parted as she had so many times before. Yet, this time, the words seemed confusing and distant. What she read made sense, yet it was as if she was hearing it from high up in a church balcony, being spoken to someone else. This was not the way it was supposed to be, the effect it was meant to have. She had been faithful, at least, she believed so. Her prayers were as boundless and fervent as ever; the nasty, sickening weather had seen to that, as had the slipping mud and the clump and crack of stone-breaking hammers.

Amanda read on, wanting to rest, yet not wanting to give up on what she knew she needed. She read of dust, and laws which were unkept, of destructions and places gone to naught, without sight or hope of redemption. Strength would be stolen, choices made, decisions irreversible, a damnation set in burning stone. All the world would be turned to turmoil and righteous souls were sold for silver, and the poor for pairs of shoes. Why did she need to know this? Why did it matter to her? What purpose was there in these words so suddenly and randomly presented to her in the hour of her need.

Closing her eyes, and pressing her palms to her face, Amanda pressed on. She turned the weathered pages yet again. Her eyes rested on a word, a scripture which seemed to fit.

When he giveth quietness, who then can make trouble? And when he hideth his face, who then can behold him? Whether it be done against a nation, or against a man only.

While contemplating this set truth, she saw the note which she had saved before. Yet it was not her note. The paper was different. It was cleaner, clearer, as if written with a firm steady hand, a hand which was not aching and afflicted with bleeding blisters. It was the writing of another, yet it bore her name. It was addressed to her.

Hesitantly, fearfully, she unfolded the pale, white half-sheet. Squinting in the flaring fire-light, she examined what had been written. The author seemed to be a man, a man named Gillean. Whoever he was, he apparently had read her letter. He claimed to be from another place, somewhere far away. She did not know if it was the place she had once inhabited, the world of her failure, yet she assumed so. He claimed to have seen her, to have been granted a vision from the Father. This made her nervous.

Who was this Gillean? It seemed too much to believe that he was where he said he was, and especially that he was now in the place that she had hitherto been. Whoever he was, he knew far too much about her. This was a trick, a devilish plot to overthrow her mind. She was in one of Hector's illusions, a cruel ploy plotted for some depraved end, and she was playing right into his twisted hands.

Yet, for all these thoughts, Amanda could not throw the stinging sense of ambivalence, the feeling that the mysterious writer might have written truth. Suffering as her faith currently was, she decided she would practice it. She would trust her Lord to show her the truth. If it was a deception, what could she do about it. If she played along and did not question what was sent her, the deceiver might tip his hand in time. That was his weakness: pride, arrogant overconfidence.

Remembering former truths learned through pain, she understood it was unwise to speak with devils. Yet she felt no distress or further uneasiness about penning an answer. Taking her time, Amanda took up her fountain pen as she had before. As the restless rain continued to pour, she responded to what this Gillean had left for her. She questioned him, asking him about himself, pressing him in every other sentence for information and details which might shed light upon his existence and the world which was his home. If this was all a lie, it would not matter. But if there was truth...But how could she be sure? Again, her Lord, the Father would have to show her.

Though she was sure regarding the matter of her response, she felt a crippling doubt welling up within her mind. This time, it did not concern the secret correspondent, but the Father himself. She realized this and struggled against it, pushing it away, trying to expel it before it was allowed take root. She could not doubt or distrust her God. He was the one who gave her life. He had always sustained her, even through her bitter and lonely days. In her trials, He had comforted her. Amanda would not doubt or question his sovereign now, she could not. What would He think of her for even permitting these thoughts to linger?

Like a dull, clammy knife, the whispers of a harassing spirit scraped against her consciousness. They burned and lingered like ant bites, taking their toll even as she rebuked the unseen foe. Try as she might, she could not shut out these foreign misgivings. Though she rebelled against them, they fed her fears. They cut deep, searching for that long-buried distress which lay hidden within. Her spirit was under attack.

So, you would place your hope and faith in someone you cannot see. How long? How long will you continue to repeat your follies? What a sad thing to see, a woman so consumed by her failures that she is forced to turn once again to the fairytales of her youth. You should be endeavoring to deliver yourself from this mess you've made. You should be clearing your mind, not trusting in someone who does not exist. Your delusion has left you all alone with this silly book. Cast it away. Cast it away and open yourself to true wisdom.

Resisting the spirit of oppression, Amanda called out to the Father. She was weary still, yet she refused to be overwhelmed. She knew on whom she believed, and she knew the truth and power, the profound security retained within his holy name. Madness and derision would not consume her so easily. Her God had promised never to leave her nor forsake her and this was something on which she must fully depend. It had been written in stone.

Lifting her eyes, she saw the demon. It held the form of an owl. Gray and glowering, it stared down on her from the crooked ceiling. Malice flowed from its yellow eyes as it attempted to manipulate both thought and emotion. Its talons clutched the rotting beams and its feathers seemed to seep an odious hubris. From its air of indignance, she assumed it had no intention to depart. This she would not abide.

"Be gone, foul creature. Leave now in the name of the Father! Depart in the sacred name of Jesus!" She cried these last words, her face flinching as tears of fear and sadness stung at her cheeks. The thing had brought with it a feeling of loneliness and isolation. The sensation lingered so strongly that she thought it would suffocate her in her grief.

With a hissing shriek, the great owl beat its wings. It swooped from off its perch and glided down, landing just shy of the door. It hopped forward as if dazzled, its dark and awful beak clicking and clacking in frustration. Striking the cracked wood with a massive talon, it exited out into the storm, swiveling its head as it left to give one last menacing glance.

Amanda breathed a sigh of relief, yet it was short-lived. The distressing emotions persisted, continuing to hound her from within. She could hear the sound of giant wings striking with the sodden air. They sounded like the throb of drums, dancing, churning out a deadly rhythm against her soul. The demon was circling the hovel, flying against the wind and rain.

There was a gut-wrenching crash, and she knew he was on the roof. He would remain there for the rest of the night, silent, yet unmoving. All Amanda could do was watch and pray. She would resolve to begin a fast and to search the depths of her heart. If there was any wicked way within her, she asked that it be removed. She was of the Father, yet she needed to draw closer unto Him. She needed to be healed.

Chapter Twelve:
A Place of Madness

After leaving behind the ravine and its sad collection of bones, Gillean's senses were heightened. They had dismounted, continuing on foot and allowing the mare to rest. Mathias led her as they walked. Gillean had felt her beginning to weaken. She was weary and in desperate need of water as were they. There was a spring at the base of these hills. It flowed out into the lowlands bordering the southern moor. God willing, they would make camp there tonight, but first they had to pass from the shadow of these rocks.

As they began their descent along the southern slopes, Gillean became aware of a growing unease. It mounted in his blood, tickling and tingling through his core until it could not be ignored. Every muscle was tightening, tensing as if in preparation for an assault. It hardened itself against some unseen evil, more aware in its own flesh than the spirit it sought to protect. The whelming apprehension was disquieting to say the least. He looked over at Mathias, checking to see if he perceived the same.

The young pastor had, until recently, been attempting to make conversation. Yet, suddenly, he had fallen silent. His thoughts had been stifled, cut off in the course of their forming. Looking back at those craggy, black peaks, he was overwhelmed by the feeling that this place might have ears. In fact, he was almost positive it did. It was as if those misty pinnacles were listening, watching, and taking note of all they said and did, attentive to their every movement. It was a leering and rotten feeling, as if someone had cut him open and was peering inside his chest. Something in the way they loomed made it almost look like they were frowning down on them. Mathias's inner child was tugging at his soul, begging him vehemently not to look back again, pleading with him to flee.

"Get yourself out of here," it said. "Something's not right. Go quickly! Do not tary! If you tary, it will overtake you. It will keep you here forever, just like the bones of those lost children. Yours shall surely lie amongst them if you do not hurry! Hurry! Hurry! Make haste, lest you be taken here and your soul be lost to wander forever in the gap! It draweth nigh! Hurry!"

It was all he could do to keep from bolting, to stop himself from lunging past Gillean and flinging himself down the slope. This seemed one terror his faith could not overcome. In front of him, he heard Gillean whisper, almost a hiss in the ominous stillness.

"It will be all right. It shall be well. We will make it through, just don't stop." He wanted to say don't look back or turn around, but he knew if he did, Mathias surely would.

"Keep your feet moving and think of the sun. Think of the Father and his love, yet do not drop your guard."

"Will there be a trap? Will we be ambushed?" Mathias said, trying to disguise the worry in his voice.

"I don't know," said Gillean. "It's hard to say. What I am sure of is that our presence here is not appreciated by something. I sense is that it would harm or imprison us if it had the chance. Let us pray it does not get the chance. Just keep moving. God willing, we'll be free of this place by nightfall."

"And if we are not?" This time, Mathias could not hide the tremble. Evening was not far off.

Gillean did not want to answer. He did not want to consider the fearful possibility of being caught in this place after dark. It would spell their doom. He did not know what "it" was, or even if "it" had a plan for their demise. He assumed a hostile spirit or dark force was what hunted them, something more than merely physical.

Gillean had been overcome with a sensation like this before. The dark feelings were both familiar and foreign, like sweet wine mixed with a rancid tonic. It was similar to the aura preceding the arrival of the gray Mavarians, yet he had encountered them enough to know when they were near. Their distinct, musty odor could be smelt for miles, and the glow projected by their sorcery was absent here.

The only thing present, which did sometimes accompany them, was the cold. The temperature had dropped. It was freezing. Gillean could not feel the icy sting on his fingers and the raw rasp of its burn inside his lungs. The air was becoming thinner now, tighter, less much less agreeable to their exertions. This made no sense, seeing as the elevation had decreased. Yet, the strange occurrence persisted.

Every breath was a half-breath now. It was as if oxygen was being stolen from them, snatched away even as they sucked it in. The effect was dizzying. It progressed in ebbing constriction, threatening to rob them of their balance and vision. If it continued, its cruel deprivation would send them tottering into fits of syncope and delirium. They had to hurry. This place was suffocating them.

In his dazed stumbling, Gillean remembered stories which the old people had told. They had alluded to the dark and mystic subject matter in hushed tones. They never mentioned them in the light of day, always at night, usually gathered about a blazing fire. They had spoken of places left behind, habitations of ancient races and forgotten kingdoms. These kingdoms, these long-abandoned domains had been changed, altered by forces unknown. They had somehow been able to transverse what was known as "the cycle," the progression of worldly dimensions. Somewhere, between the destruction of their time and the beginning of the new, they had been hidden, covered over to continue on. These were set aside by some strange happenstance or curse.

These realms were suspended, never moving forward nor able to revert. They were caught in the midst, prisoners of what had been and outcasts to what now was. According to the sages of his youth, places such as these were not suitable for mortal life. They were not compatible with flesh and blood. Oh, you could pass through, even camp within their midst, yet woe betide any who chose to linger.

The curses of the trapped realms ran deep. In most cases, their enmity was strong as well, so vehement, in fact, that it was capable of corrupting the soundest mind and most noble heart. These were the strongholds of demons. The old people had called them "habitations of owls," for the owl had long been the symbol of the "Watchers," dark spirits which had long tormented man. These demons dealt in deceit and manipulation. They were said to be capable of turning a man's thoughts and emotions against him.

Time was when Gillean had disregarded the words of his elders. He had overlooked them, pushing them aside as merely scary stories, the kind told to frighten children into behaving, to keep them from wandering off. Yet, now he knew better. These stories were not just stories after all. Most hid subtle, yet undeniable, truths. Others were, and remained, just as vividly real as the day they had occurred and been recorded.

Gillean had seen at least two of these remnant realms first hand. He had entered them unaware and woefully unprepared. His stupidity and foolishness had not only placed him in mortal danger, it had led another to her death. His blindness had cost a faithful friend her life, a woman whom he believed had truly loved him; in some ways more than his estranged wife ever had.

Gillean was determined to learn from his tragic mistakes. He still blamed himself for much of the misfortunes of his past. He knew full well he could not change them, yet had sworn to take what he had learned and apply it. They had to get out of here.

Despite their struggle to breathe, the two men found themselves running for their lives. They leapt and bounded down the slanting slopes. The horse followed hard upon their heels, just as eager to escape as they.

An unholy wind welled up behind them. It was not of the desert or of a storm from the east. It howled and gusted at its own volition, tearing at their backs and spitting ice against their necks. It was a gale of madness. It screamed and railed against them, the hillside, and all that drew breath. Like a lion, it pounced again and again, nearly toppling them to their deaths. It truly seemed as if this was its intent.

The wild rage did not abate till they had reached level ground. Only then did its howling cease and its torrents subside. At last, they had made it through. Still, they kept fleeing, not slowing till they reached the spring. The sound of its bubbling flow did wonders for their nerves. The mare put her head down and began to drink, taking great gulps of the lifegiving liquid. Gillean and Mathias both drank as well. They filled three canteens and Gillean's water-balloon, before setting up camp.

Mathias helped to gather what sparse kindling he could find. When Gillean's back was turned, he finally gave in to the impulse to look back and survey the dark peaks.

In the depths of evening, the Spiderback hills remained shrouded in mists. They looked more haunting and forbidding than ever. In the shadows cut into the space between the peaks, he thought he saw a pair of eyes, yellow and glowering. They were the eyes of an owl: an owl wishing their hurt.

Mathias wanted to tell Gillean what he had seen, but decided against it. Praying to the Father, he tried to force the image out of his mind. They were well away. It could not harm them now. Besides, God would protect them. He has bigger than any demon and more than able to conquer and bind the devil in chains unto the day of final reckoning. Greater was He who was in them than he who was in this world. Perhaps they would still be able to sleep tonight.

Chapter Thirteen:
Hector's Return

Amanda's illness was growing steadily worse. She was still able to work, but only just. Her strength was beginning to fail her, and her fits of coughing were becoming increasingly more violent. They were about to tear her apart.

She remembered all the times she had been sick before. In the past, before this cursed existence, she had always been able to rest and recover. She had taken this for granted, yet now, she fully understood the blessing a day of inactivity could be. Rest was the key. It was essential to survival and remaining in good health. Yet, even when Amanda was able to sleep, she was always awakened to the beating wings of that horrible bird, the owl which now lived upon her roof.

Amanda had prayed for it to depart, ceaselessly petitioning the Father to remove it. It had not budged. The wretched creature seemed neither to eat nor sleep. It only watched, staring with its ghastly golden eyes. These appeared able to cut through all things. They did not close or waver; they burned. She could feel them as she slept, counting her ragged breaths, probing her heart. The creature was testing her, she thought. It was prying at the edge of her sanity, attempting to ascertain how much more it would take to break her, to make her go insane.

Amanda continued to immerse herself in the Word. Even in her failing health, it was a continual comfort to her. Though understanding was not always easy, she was finding it less difficult to trust her God. She knew that she had not been abandoned. Her hope was not determined by emotions or by what could be seen. It lived in the life she had been given, and in the comfort of the still, small voice.

He spoke to her now, more than ever. He was her rescue, aiding her in moments unlooked for. There were times in which Amanda felt she surely would have collapsed, had not His good grace upheld her, giving her strength hitherto unknown. God had promised her that she would live. He had done so through the written words of the stranger.

She knew now that Gillean was not a deception; he was real. Though far removed by distance, and perhaps even time, he had as much life and breath as she. He had answered her question with a patient grace, telling not only of himself, but of the world she had once known.

When she was first taken, it had been on a downward spiral. Yet now, it seemed things had become far bleaker. Another conflict had ravaged the lands, destroying the cities and wiping out millions. The poisons in the soil had not been diluted. They had persisted in the stifling of green and growing life, and had created new deserts, wastelands in which hardly anything could live. The sun had not returned to the sky. The dimmed light of day was still a mockery. Yet, hope remained, for there were still some who reverenced the name of the Father.

The man Gillean seemed concerned for her. He had promised to pray for her preservation. He said that he would try and find a way to rescue her, though she knew not how he could. Even if it were within the ability of a mortal man, Hector would stand in the way.

Gillean seemed to know him, this man who dressed in darkness. He said he had encountered her captor before. Hector had stolen something from him; he had, in one way or another, torn apart his life. The devilish fiend seemed to excel at that. Wherever he ventured, there was madness and despair. He was a destroyer: a lying, deceiving thief whose only true purpose was to inflict chaos.

Where had he come from, this evil apparition of the night? It was clear that he was no mortal man, yet, neither was he fully demon. Perhaps he was the devil himself, the antipathy of the Father incarnate. Whatever his origins, Amanda was forced to admit she was afraid of him.

Still mindful to pace herself, Amanda put her back into her work. When she made it back to her dwelling, she would write to Gillean again. She would tell him once more of this place and what surrounded her. Maybe there were details she was missing, something which she had overlooked that he might be able to point out. She believed God had given him discernment and anointing. Surely, he would help her. He would do his best.

Amanda knew she as in the Father's hand, yet the thought of dying here set her teeth on edge. The unpleasant possibility sent shivers down her spine and caused a cold sweat to gather on her brow. She must escape, and soon. This place was not her home, and she would not resign herself to its persistent torments.

Just then, her skin crawled and her stomach plunged. Amanda reeled and became dizzyingly week. Dropping her rock-hammer, she staggered back, panting for breath. Her heart lurched and she felt as if she was about to pass out. Her faltering movements caught the eye of an overseer, a particularly mean brute with a bullwhip clenched in his fist. He bellowed and moved towards her, the sinews on his bare back and neck flexing in grotesque rhythm.

This was it. There would be no escape. He would break her neck and beat her into the mud. The curling bullwhip quivered and thrashed as the goliath allowed it to uncoil. He raised his spring-loaded arm, preparing to strike. Yet the blow never came.

Opening her feverish eyes, which she had squinched shut in preparation of the pain, Amanda gasped. She had been spared from one danger, yet it seemed another had swooped in to take its place.

Hovering not five feet away was none other than the elusive Hector. A sneering grin was plastered across his face and he looked younger, bolder than she had ever seen him. He clutched the back of the overseer's neck with his hand, causing the man to grimace in pain. The scene was almost comical. Though Hector was tall, his form was so much smaller than the burly behemoth, yet he clearly held the man's life in his hand.

The tall man laughed. As one might flick away an insect, Hector turned and tossed away the overseer. There was a distant crash as the flying guard collided with the treetops. Then, there was silence.

Amanda's vision blurred, then dimmed. She felt her legs buckle beneath her and she collapsed, fading into nothingness. As the last rays of quivering shade fled her view, she heard Hector's sing-song voice.

"Sleep now, child. Sleep deep. Cast away your foolish hopes and dreams. I shall give you new ones. Sleep safely and know, when you choose to wake, I shall still remain."

Chapter Fourteen:
The Cackling Man

"What are you doing?" Mathias asked, peering at the older man, with a look both curious and concerned.

Any other might have been offended at the pastor's prying, yet Gillean was not. He answered him without looking up, his mind still fixed upon the growing content of the paper.

"A letter. One long overdue. I'm sending it to someone in great need."

"Who?" Mathias queried.

"Her name is Amanda. She is far away. Yet, soon, she may be going on a journey."

"Does the poste still run through where we are headed?"

"We shall surely see."

Gillean was not yet ready to tell this man about his correspondence by way of the Word. He perceived Mathias to be an openminded man, yet, some things just sounded too crazy. At times, Gillean still struggled to convince himself that this was real. He found himself compelled to write, moved by the Spirit of the Father from the deepest foundations of his heart. He found it strange; he hardly knew the woman for which he prayed, yet he felt as if he somehow did. It was as if he had known her for years, had spoken with her, had walked with her through the turmoil of this shattered earth. Between his dreams and the continued letters, it felt as though she were apart of him. Though they remained distant, they were close, and growing closer. Mystery of mysteries, what had the Father purposed?

As Gillean finished his letter and committed it to the pages of the Father's Word, Mathias began to hum. It was an old tune, and sacred, one which had been sung long ago by Gillean's father. Slowly, methodically, the words fell into place. They rose up with the sparks of the campfire to grace the darkened sky.

"When the world turns slow to the foolish and vain,
When the laughter of men mocks the child in pain,
When the tree will not grow,
When the evil winds blow,
It is time, it is time, it is time.
It is time for the Lord to return,
Lest the faith should be scattered and wrongfully spurned.
In the One we shall trust,
He shall not forsake us.
It is time, it is time, it is time."

They sang in unison under the stars. Their voices carried on the wind. It was good to sing old songs such as these. Doing so was a balm to the soul. It took away their fear, rebuking the darkness and drawing light into their souls. But these emotions did not last.

No sooner had their singing cease, than ghoulish laugher split the night. Both men jumped up. Gillean grabbed for his revolver and Mathias the short-barreled rifle. Their nerves taut, they scanned the darkness, looking for a target.

In another moment, they saw the author of the voice. He was a wild man, clothed in skins and caked in dust. His eyes were blossoms of madness, glowing in the firelight. He had crept up close on silent feet. He had listened to them and their song, somehow managing to keep his peace until the end. Gillean could tell this man was a desert dweller, most likely an outcast, a fugitive ostracized from the lands of the living.

The man laughed again, letting loose a long profane cackle, choked on the end of it and began to cough, spluttering and flailing at his chest. He spit and then turned back to them, his new grin more imbecilic than his first.

"A fine night! A fine night to you gentlemen! O, ho, ho, yes! A fine night for a sing. What brings you to these dusty stomping ground, eh? What brings you out here?"

"Our business is our business. We are headed south. What do you mean by approaching our camp so in the dead of night, cackling like a mad man? Stay your insanity and leave us in peace!"

GIllean kept one eye and his gun fixed on the intruder, yet all the while, he searched the gloom. This could very well be a distraction. The nomad seemed truly deranged, yet, if this was a ploy, they would need to know it soon. Their lives might depend on it.

The lunatic continued on as if he had not heard him. "I is Kedder, Kedder Milbin. I means no harm, certainly not. I wa just out for a stroll this essistential evening and decided to pay my respects."

"In the name of the Father, depart."

"I an't no demon if that's what yur thinkin. I don't skitter at the Father's name, bless his soul. I just takin my time, tryin to understand what type of peoples you is."

"The type that want to be left in peace."

"I see so, I see so." The Kedder chortled, "Yet such as all things, peace comes at a price. You got any vittles about ya?"

Mathias looked over at Gillean. He could read what the pastor was thinking through his eyes, yet he disagreed. If they fed this imbecile, he would never leave them. He would follow them like a sick dog, hounding them until he died.

"We have to show the Love of the Father," the younger man said, lowering his weapon. "Otherwise, what good are we to this world?"

Begrudgingly, Gillean relented. He gave a nod at which Mathias went over and retrieved some dried meat from the satchel. He poured some water into a small, tin cup and carried the items out towards the raving man. He set them down on a stone and stepped back.

Kedder pounced upon the victuals. With ravenous hunger he consumed them, gulping down the water and tearing through the meat, his chipped teeth clicking as he ate. Only when it was gone did he turn his attentions back to them.

"I thank thee my children. I thank thee. That were just what this ole frame needed."

Before Gillean could tell him to hush, Mathias spoke again. "We are headed for the trading post on the edge of the dead-lands, it's just south of here. You are more than welcome to accompany us there."

At this the man's glowing eyes widened and his form stiffened. He stumbled back and began to howl. Gillean cocked the hammer on his revolver.

"Now ole Gaven post! No! No! Not goin back! No! Never. There be evil thar! Eeeeveeel! You find a demon there sure enough! Ghostly lights and rotten bone! Be gone! Be gone from these cursed lands lest you be overcome by the five! The five have awoken! B'ware! B'ware!"

And with that he ran off, howling into the night. They watched him go with bewilderment. Gillean was relieved, yet also a tad fearful. What had the old nomad meant? The post was called Gaven post, and it was not known for its upright dealings, yet what was there which caused this man to howl? What demon did he speak of and who were "the five"?

They did not let their guard down for some time after that. The old man's words haunted them. They were inane and possibly of little or no consequence, yet they remained, chillingly set within their minds.

In his soul, Gillean sensed the dread from the hills beginning to return. There was something more to this than just the night wind and the memory of babblings. He realized the nomad had believed everything he spoke. Perhaps there was something at the Gaven trading post, something it would be best to avoid. Yet they had come so far. Tomorrow they would reach it and would discern for themselves if it was safe. For now they would sleep, or at least try. They would take turns keeping watch until daybreak. He prayed it would come swiftly.

Chapter Fifteen:
The Irrational Curse

When morning finally came, Gillean rose early. He was still tired from the events of the night before, yet tried to hide this behind a mask of firm resolve. His companion could not however. Mathias yawned and rubbed his eyes, blinking sleepily long after they had gotten underway.

They continued along on foot. They followed the stream, keeping abreast of the wide moor stretching out to their west. Their mare was still weak. Now and again, she stumbled, almost tripping over her own hooves. Her coat had long since lost its softness and was beginning to patch and thin. Gillean had hoped fresh water would help her, yet this had not been the case. The horse hung its head as it labored on, and her eyes were lined with a glossy, yellow sheen. It might not be long before they lost her.

They saw no sign of the cackling man, not footprint, nor leaving. He had vanished as if flown away on the wind. Gillean guessed he had fled east across the stream, back towards the dusty deserts to the east. He truly hoped they would not encounter him again. Something in the man's glowing, animal eyes made his skin crawl. Most likely, the fool was just a drifter, too long isolated and acquainted with the poisons and voices of the wasteland.

As the stream narrowed and dried up, they began to notice the wreckage lining the horizon. The massive hulls and husks of crippled air-ships stood aloof beneath the chalk dust sky. Their metal armor was tarnished, faded and covered in a concealment of gray grime.

Spent shell casings crunched and clicked beneath their feet. This had once been the scene of a battle, possibly one of the final clashes between the Assembly and the Sons of Veritas. Gillean doubted there was now anyone left to tell the tale. Maybe a few battle-scarred, Assembly soldiers, or a crippled fugitive survivor. Possibly the old man might have been able to enlighten them.

Gillean pondered concerning what they had lost. He thought of all the knowledge which had been stripped away and buried with all those long-forgotten dead. Would anyone ever reclaim it? Would they be permitted to, and if so, would they have time? He doubted it. The time for that was past, he thought, as he kicked away a rusted shell. This world had had it chance. It had been granted plenty of them, more than mortal sanity could fathom. Surely God's ways were higher than his, and for this he was thankful.

Mathias was beginning to lag behind. He had never been able to shake the weariness with which he had woken. He was stumbling along now, seemingly with less stamina than even the dying horse. He seemed ragged and pitiful, swaying and only half-sure of his movements.

Gillean looked back at him, and suddenly stopped. He had seen something move against the ground. A small beast had darted across the path behind them and had disappeared into the rocks of the dry riverbed. It had looked like a cat, small and nimble with yellowish fur and black stripes running along its back. Gillean knew of no such creature inhabiting these lands. There were cats in the north, but they were all black, living mostly in abandoned towns and cities.

He did not ponder over this for long. The day was wearing on, and they were not making good time. Mathias slipped on the uneven ground, and Gillean fixed his eyes on him. Instead of realizing the man was in trouble, Gillean began to judge him for his slowness.

He has had more rest than I, he thought. *Why is he slowing us down? Why am I even permitting him to travel with me.* Gillean had business to attend to, and the last thing he needed was to be encumbered by this lost, careless "holy man", if that was really what he was.

Suspicion and paranoia grew inside him. They took root and flowered like scurrilous, poisonous plants. Their razor barbs probed deep, inflicting wounds within his mind.

How had Mathias really defeated those ravenous wolves? For someone fleeing for his life, he certainly had very little fear. Not even Gillean had reached that level of faith. The closer he looked at Mathias, the more eerily familiar he seemed: familiar and odious, as if he were a character from one of his nightmarish dreams. Perhaps he was. The dazed man's tattered, black robes cause him to appear as a specter, transcendent of this withered world.

Suddenly, it dawned on him. Their meeting had been no mere happenstance. This man was Hector, his old, ghostly foe returned to hinder him. He was following along behind, feigning weakness, yet was surely leading Gillean into a trap. This would not do. Gillean had fallen prey to the dark man's guiles before. He would not allow himself to be ensnared again.

Drawing out his slide-bolt pistol, Gillean moved towards Mathias. So intent was he on his target, that he did not see the small ocelot creep silently from the gulch and hover in the shadow of his boot. Its dim, golden eyes flickered as if they were not real. The big man had become careless. Though he labored along; in his mind he had become complacent.

Mathias looked up at Gillean, a look of vague surprise on his face. Gillean stopped, just outside arms reach, aiming his gun at the chest of his companion. His face was cold and hard, emotionless, as if he had no feeling left but hate. If this was Hector, then he was to blame for all the years of loss and loneliness. Today he would have his revenge.

Mathias opened his mouth as if to speak, yet words evaded him. He did not know what was happening. His vision was blurred, blinded by the hot glow of the sunless sky, which seemed to burn ever brighter. He could not think straight. Gillean was a shadow, something unreal to him. Turning his head, he began to hum as he had the night before, the tune rising and falling in strained vibrations across his lips.

As Gillean's finger grew heavy against the trigger, a jolt of pain snapped through his heart. An arrythmia jolted through his chest, forcing him back as the still, small voice resounded him his mind. Its rebuke was a shock and a relief all at once. It was like cold water after a burning flame, yet stung like salt pressed into a wound.

That was the moment the ocelot pounced. Hissing, it sunk its teeth and claws into the leather of Gillean's boot. Instantly, there was a blinding flash as its venom entered his blood.

Gillean kicked and thrashed at the evil creature, attempting to free himself from its poison grasp. Regaining his senses, Mathias gave a yell and rushed towards him. Knocking Gillean over, he grabbed for the knife which hung from his belt. Seizing hold of the handle, he snatched it from its sheath even as his leg was knocked out from under him by a stray kick.

Sprawling beside his fallen friend, for he truly considered him so, Mathias jabbed wildly at the creature. He prayed through clenched teeth as he struggled to see and the blade connected with the cat's side. The demonic beast released Gillean's boot and let forth a screeching cry. It turned on Mathias his shoulders coiled and mouth open. It crouched to spring, but never did. A well-aimed hoof crushed it into the ground. The horse had ended their struggle with one sudden stomp.

"What was that?" Mathias gasped, wriggling back and struggling to stand.

"Something bad," said Gillean.

He grimaced and clutched his boot. The cat's fangs had punched small, uneven holes in the leather. From the burning coursing up his leg, he knew the bite had been venomous. Pulling off his boot and the ratty sock beneath it, he inspected the wounds. There were two punctures to his lower ankle, from which the blood still trickled freely. The surrounding skin was blanched and marred by purple streaks which crisscrossed each other like opposing claws of lightning. The site was beginning to swell.

Mathias had pulled himself up and was feverishly rummaging through Gillean's pack, looking for something which might help him. Gillean hissed to him and he looked up in alarm.

"There's a small, metal tube, no bigger than a saltshaker. I need it."

Mathias continued to search frantically, yet he could not locate the item in question. After a half minute, he gave up and hefted the pack over to Gillean. He tore into it, his hands trembling. The pain screamed out, racing up his leg and twisting into his flank. With a half-suppressed snarl, he threw down the pack, and snatched up his canteen. His venom extractor was gone. He had remembered packing it, yet now it was not there. Of all the infernal foolishness!

He washed the wounds with warm water. The punctured area had stiffened and was turning red, yet the purple threads had spread no further. He hoping this was a good sign.

Gillean gritted his teeth, pulled his sock back on, and forced his boot over the worrisome site. He looked back over at his companion and saw Mathias staring dumbfounded at the place where the ocelot had been. It was gone. The ground was trampled and depressed in the grainy ground where the mare had flattened it, yet no sign of the thing remained.

"It just vanished!" Mathias said. "It fell to bits and became like dust, drifting away on the wind."

"If was never really dead, just disembodied. It may return."

"You mean..."

"Yes. It was a demon."

"Why didn't either of us sense its presence? That of the evil in the hills was so strong."

"We have both been weary. I don't know about you, but I think I let that old man get to me, I let him and his words linger in my head. We should have renewed our minds before departing. We should not have been in such a hurry, and should have been more mindful of our focus."

"What about your leg?" He paused, looking down at Gillean's blood-stained boot. "You should ride. I can keep on walking."

"I'll manage," Gillean said gruffly. "If it gets too painful, I might, but I don't think I'll die from this today, something tells me I won't. Presently, I think you need to be the one on the horse. You almost fell out back there."

Gillean had just now realized that Mathias had been unaware of the events transpiring prior to the creature's attack. The fact that Gillean had, not seven minutes ago, held a gun on him, seemed to have evaded him. It was as if caught, deep within a trance. Gillean considered recounting the full story and asking the man's forgiveness; yet he decided against this. It would be best just to let this one lie. Hopefully, they would leave the irrational curse behind them in this weary and wasted place.

    They were almost to their destination. The trading post could not be much more than seven or eight miles south of here. 'Ere long, they would find one of the old roads and would follow it the rest of the way. They would arrive by nightfall.

    Mathias, having still retained some of his pride, refused to ride. He made it clear that he intended to keep close watch over Gillean, for the sake of his safety, of course. Gillean wondered if this was the real reason. Still, he did not want to argue. They rested a bit longer and drank deeply from their canteens before moving on, also refreshing themselves in the Word of the Father.

    Later, as he staggered on, Gillean notice that the pain in his leg had begun to grow numb. Its burn had diminished, yet he did not doubt for a moment that the poison was still there. He had been afflicted like this once before; not from a bite, but from a bullet, a poisoned bullet bewitched with a spirit of bitterness. This was not the type of infirmity which could be healed with medicine, at least not fully. This was a toxin which clung to the soul. Only time would reveal of its true effects. He prayed the Father would provide a remedy.

Chapter Sixteen:
Resisting Medicine

In the world of her dreams, Amanda could be sure of nothing. The flow and pulse of jumbled thoughts coursed above and beneath her, winding on like the intricacies of a many-colored quilt. It moved, yet she did not move with it. She felt far removed. She was only a spectator, a witness to its ever-changing tides.

The first clear image she saw, the first one she could easily believe, was that of a beach. The shoreline stretched out in a long and waving line of soft, cream-colored sand, broken only by the gentle wash of waves. They curled and glided, whispering softly as they rose and fell. Their grays and blues were the hues and shades of cooled morning. The aroma was that of brine mixed with the sweetness of sun-kissed sand. It was the smell of joy.

Overhead, the gulls and cormorants cried and called. They chased each other on the wind. All was both peaceful and blissful. All was safe. She was the only living human for miles.

There was loneliness here, yet there was also restful contentment. None could harm her where she stood. She was safe. She was secure. They sky, and sand, and rolling waves were all she needed.

"Turn around."

The command reverberated in her mind as loud and clear as if it had been spoken in her ear. Amanda turned and saw a marvelous sight.

Moving towards her, its fine main flowing in the breeze, was the most beautiful horse she had ever seen. The bold stallion glided across the silky sands, shining white as could be. He was graceful as the living dawn. He had not spot nor blemish. His coat was well-groomed, pure, and even. His long, powerful legs carried him far with each stride, and his eyes: his eyes were like living fire. Strange fire which seemed to burn straight through her soul.

Amanda stood still, daring only to breathe, until the wondrous beast was directly in front of her. He lowered his massive head and gazed deep into her eyes. He appeared to be smiling, though she knew this was silly, horses could not smile. All the same, the creatures face seemed kind. The eyes, though still burning, appeared honest and polite.

The majestic creature bent its knee and tucked its head in what seemed to be a bow. Amanda wanted to bow in return, yet, something told her she should not. Her late husband had told her she should bow to none other than to her God and to her King. This horse was neither. No matter how polite, it was not worthy of the gesture.

As if able to read her thoughts, the beast spoke. "Do not fear, little one. You need not lower yourself before me. I am here to serve. I would show you the way, the path unto healing and redemption. Speak to me truthfully; do you wish to be made pure?"

Amanda was taken aback. It was such a charming voice, so gentle and full of life. It was like this place, so serine and sweet. Yet, for all its echantments, it seemed oddly out of place. A misgiving began to rise within her soul.

"Come now my child. I know your heart. It is fearfully created, yet it is dark and defiled. It must be cleansed. Please, I beg of you, allow me to enter it. I would see its beauty and virtues restored."

And with that, the face of the stallion changed. It became longer, more pronounced, yet no less graceful. From his forehead there arose a single spiraled horn. It was the color of ivory, yet it shown with the radiance of a setting sun., glistening with a rusty glow. It reminded Amanda of blood. Not living blood, but aged and stale, drawn from the heart of one who is dying.

"Allow me just one touch, oh precious one. Just one touch upon your heart and I shall make thee pure."

The tip of the horn was as sharp as a razor. It was moving closer now, closer to her chest, where her heart had begun to quiver. She wanted to draw back, to retreat, but she was frozen, her body gripped by a stone-like paralysis.

The ivory blade, for that was what it had become, was now inches from her sternum. She watched in terror as the horses' eyes flared. She had seen those burning, smoldering eyes before, and now she knew where. They were the eyes of Hector.

She was still petrified, powerless to save herself. In a blind burst of desperation, she willed her lips to move and utter the only name she could. "Jesus".

The sinister stallion jolted back as if hit in between the eyes with a branding iron. He reared and snorted, tossing his head wildly. Suddenly, Amanda was aware of another presence flitting before her eyes. It was a dove.

The stallion's voice became a shriek, then deepened into a bellow. The color of his coat changed, shifted into a dark and shadowed gray. Sparks flew from the creature's eyes, now a deadly, smoldering red. Instead of one blade, there were ten, jutting and curling like tree roots from his deformed skull. The steed had become a horror. All his deceptions had been stripped away, and he was furious.

The dove attacked, striking at the beast's blood-red eyes. The nightmare was driven back. He belched flame and vomited brimstone, yet the pure power held him at bay. "You will never win," the dove seemed to be saying, "There is one far greater than thou shall ever be."

The terrifying monster made one last lunge for Amanda, his mouth open, his teeth like chunks of black granite rushing towards her. In the same instant, the holy dove dived at him. There was a burst of light followed by what could only be described as a boom which shook heaven and earth.

Amanda was jolted into wakefulness. She was in a bed, her head against a sweat-soaked goose-down pillow. The light from a nearby fire cast dancing shadows against the ceiling.

Hector lay against the far wall where he had landed, fallen in a disgruntled heap. He seemed rattled, shaken by what had befallen him. Amanda guessed that he was not accustomed to being told no.

As he rose, the dark man seemed to regain some of his composure. He stood tall, his form shifting and twisting with the writhing of the shadows. He approached her bed slowly, methodically. His smoldering eyes narrowed, looking for all the world like those of a schoolmaster about to chide a disrespectful pupil

"So, this is how you treat your healer, the one who would make you well. You are unwise to resist my medicines, fair one. They could do you a world's worth of good."

"You are not my healer." Amanda's voice was weak, yet she gained strength from the Spirit of the Father. "I know on whom I have believed and am persuaded that He is able to keep that which I have committed unto Him against that day."

"You know not of what you speak." Hector hissed, drawing in close, the shadows riming around his eyes. I have seen the day. I live in anticipation of it. It is the day when mortal man shall be called unto account and he shall burn within the fires of his own sin. Who do you think that I am, the origin of evil? Nay, I am but a watcher, a prophet of the doom which is to come. The only way to escape from the wrath of him who sits above is through me. I alone know the secrets of his mind. You call him a father, yet you know nothing of him. We see through a glass darkly. All you know is what he has told you. Do you really expect the man holding all the cards to be honest? What I'm offering is better that his best and most creative illusions. Fly with me and you shall not only be healed, you shall be free, free to do as your heart desires. All you must do is to kiss my ring."

Hector held out his right hand, a dark-red ruby catching the light of the flames. She looked at him and then closed her eyes. The pain and fever were pressing in on her. The crush of a thousand migraines gripped her skull and Amanda knew not whether she would live or die.

"You must think me a fool, Hector, son of the darkness. I love the Lord my God, and He only shall I serve. He is my refuge and strength, a very present help in trouble."

Hector drew back, a look of sheer disgust on his face. It lingered there for a moment more before it was replaced with a leering smirk. He threw back his head and laughed.

"You still believe He has not abandoned you. You have only deceived yourself. You are still my prisoner dear one. You will accept my offer eventually; I have seen this, and so I know. Sleep well, fair one. Sleep well and know that you will always belong to me."

Chapter Seventeen:
Gaven Post

Just as darkness was beginning to rise up around them, they saw the lights. The trading post, or Gaven post as the locals called it, lay sprawled out on the border of the dead lands. It was lit with a strange conglomerate of torches and electric lights. Cables and sagging wires hung in webbed tangles above the rooftops. From somewhere out of sight, the hum and whir of a generator kept up its fitful song. The streets were lined with splintered boards. They had been laid over the deep cracks and potholes to provide a way for walking. They cracked and creaked as the people stepped on and off of them, milling about in the flickering glow of the lights.

The place had the smell of stale bread and oily smoke. There were meals cooking in the kitchen of a ramshackle saloon, but the aroma was not in the least appealing. Gillean had learned long ago that most of the food served in this place was not to be trusted. If they intended to remain on their feet, they would stick to beans and gruel. Much of the meat would be tainted, and that which was not was of questionable origins. The thought of it would have been enough to turn his stomach, had it not already been upset.

The pain in his right leg had once again begun to throb. He feared to look at it, yet he could feel the swelling pressed tight against his boot. He would have a time getting it off. Yet, all in all, he was relieved that the poison had not sickened him more. Its effects might well intensify at any time, but he would continue to trust and pray. He told himself it was not a wound unto death. He would keep this as his hope. Gillean had healed well before, and if he must suffer, there would be a purpose even in this.

A few of the loitering persons gave a wide-eyed look at the sight of the horse. Some stared with devilish hunger in their eyes, yet none spoke out or offered greeting. They shuffled off or turned back to their compatriots, muttering in tentative tones.

Gillean and Mathias had previously spoke concerning what they would do with the mare. They could not keep the beast. They had not the wherewithal to care for it, and on the slim chance that a battalion of Assembly Guardsmen was to show up, to be caught with it might mean trouble. Selling it quickly was the best thing for all concerned.

While Mathias left him to seek out lodging for the night, Gillean saw to the business at hand. He spoke with a thick-faced man leaning against the wall of the saloon who pointed him to another man serving drinks behind the bar. Finally acquiring his attention, Gillean told him of the animal he had tied up outside. The man tried to cheat him, offering less silver than half the mare's worth. Yet, Gillean had learned to haggle. After some bargaining, they finally agreed on twelve and a half pieces of silver. Though the horse was technically contraband, this did not matter much here. Gillean knew what would be done to the animal, and he tried not to think on it. The mare had served them well and he was sorry it had come to this, but they had no other option. Turning the creature loose on the moor and in the wastelands would render the same result. The people of Gaven post would have its meat for their grills all the same, seeing that the wild dogs did not find it first.

    Taking with him the money which Gillean had given, Mathais had rented them a room in one of the local hostelries. It was like the rest of the buildings in this run-to-ruin place. It was dirty and filled with holes. If there had been rain, the riddled metal roof would have proved poor shelter; yet as it stood, the lodging would do.

    It had a single window framed by red, motheaten curtains. Two sleeping mats lay in ragged tatters on the floor, each with its almost clean blanket. There was even a wash basin and a small cast-iron cook stove in one corner, the kind which, if left untended, could burn the dried-out place to a cinder in under two minutes. The hostess had been thoughtful enough to warn them of this. It was apparent, from the scorch marks in the hallway, this establishment had suffered several close calls in the past.

For a bit more than it was worth, Gillean bought them supper, two steaming bowls of gruel, which were delivered to their room along with water and a small flask of grog. Mathias's eyes grew wide when he saw the grog, yet Gillean chuckled and was quick to reassure him. He did not drink and had no intention to start now, it was for his wound.

It took all he had in him to keep from screaming as he poured the strong substance over the inflamed site which had now turned fully purple. He briefly considered cauterizing it, yet realized this would most likely do no good. Again, the poison of this infliction was more than merely natural.

Mathias's concern had grown, and even though Gillean tried to reassure him, the persistent pastor would not relent in his chidings till he had promised to search for medicine come morning. Gillean was beginning to feel as if he were a child, and this "holy man" was bent on becoming his nanny. The feeling was grualing, yet he tolerated his friend's behavior with patience, at least he did the best he could. He could feel an anger beginning to rise up within him. It had not been there before, not like this. It was slow and seething, like molten led beneath his ribs. Thoughts of his past had begun to resurface. Images of his losses and mistreatments flashed through his mind and, try as he might, he could not shut them out, not even with the Word of the Father. The faces of past tormentors and foes harried his fitful dreams. He saw Hector, standing motionless, as dark and mocking as ever. With him was the woman of nightmares past, the old crone who had tried to strangle him, the cursed Lillith. She stood apart from Hector, yet Gillean could tell they were linked, somehow connected in the dark and weaving web of their evil.

These things worried Gillean greatly. He was sure it was the poison, the tainted flame still lingering within the circulation of his blood. He had forgiven the vile woman for all her wrongs towards him and his late wife. He had made the conscious choice to do so, knowing full well, if he did not, the Father would not forgive him of his own sins. Even so, there might be some deeper meaning to these persistent recollections, this anger burning into his mind. A warning? Possibly. Yet not all dreams were of the Father. As much as he hated to admit to it, he had left himself open to deceptions of late. Now was not the time to grow lax in his convictions. Whatever lay ahead, he must set his focus upon the one who guided and guarded his steps. He and Mathias must both remain vigilant. God willing, this thorn in his flesh would pass. Till then, he must steel his mind. He must continue on in what he had been shown and taught. When he was stronger, he would complete his business and leave this shady place. It felt safer than the Spiderback hills, yet there was a dimness here, a darkness which preyed upon his already burdened mind, feeding his unrest and aiding the infection which threatened the integrity of his soul. It would be good when the time came to depart. If they lingered, this place would only give them trouble.

Chapter Eighteen:
Departed Friends

Alone, Gillean walked the shaded woods and latent fields of his past. He knew not that he was dreaming, nor would he have cared to know. He only knew that he was lost, and the world which he had loved lay in disarray.

The towering trees hung over him, their boney fingers reaching down. They clawed the fitful wind, spastic and writhing as he past. They were barren, as much as they had ever been, yet the lower growth still had its life. The weeds and bushes rose in thick tangle to become as walls. Their dark and close-knit stems closed in about him as if to ensnare him.

Gillean felt distant from everything, including himself. It was as if he wandered in search of his soul, as if it had fled from him, taking refuge in some distant place. Yet he knew this was not why he walked.

He was searching for his friends, the companions of his youth. These were the ones who understood him, who knew him for who he truly was, who had seen his heart. In times past, he had journeyed with them in both darkness and light, in sunshine and in rain. He had come to regarded them as brothers, valuing their lives before his own.

Gillean knew they valued him; this knowledge was planted securely in his soul. In every season they had remained devout, regardless of their quarrels or distress. They had always looked out for each other, except for now. Now they had vanished.

    He felt sure they were somewhere in this place, this sprawling wilderness with its giant trees and mossy growth. Gillean did not know where he was, yet he was guided by his gut, a fixed feeling in his bones. If he pressed on, he would surely find them. They would be gathered just ahead of him, somewhere in this silent place. Any moment now, he would walk up on them and they would turn and greet him, joking and laughing as once they had. He looked forward to speaking with them again, his heart was set on it. It felt like ages since they had talked. There was so much he had to tell them, so many thoughts, feelings, and knowings bounding inside of him. He wanted to hear from each of them as well. What had transpired in their lives? What stories did they have to tell?

    Up ahead, the trees and hedges fell away into open ground. Hurrying, Gillean made for it without hesitation. He thought he could see movement between the sandy trunks. Rounding the last bit of obscuring brush, he stepped out into the open. He looked up and felt a cold fist slam into his heart.

They were all here, just as he had known they would be, and yet, they were not. They were silent and motionless, frozen against a gray stone wall which bordered the clearing. They hung by their necks, lifeless in this awful, empty place. In that moment, Gillean realized he would never again hear their voices, and the agony of this thought was almost more than he could bear.

He shuffled past them, one by one, the only soul in attendance at this solemn wake. As he did, he spoke their names; Steven, Dathan, Judah, Roger, Bradon. He spoke softly, reverently with tears welling in his eyes. He tried to recall the good times, the things about them which had made them who they were. Yet all he could see was their faces, cold and sullen in the grasp of death.

Slowly, the memory returned to him. They had all perished years hence, executed by the forces of the Assembly. They had been captured all together. These had been peaceful men, not affiliated with any form of resistance, yet this had not mattered. The soldiers had taken none of their silver or their gold. They had never given them time to speak. There had been no trial, no chance for them to clear themselves. They had been hung as an example, a warning to all those who lived beneath the heel of oppression.

In the name of God they had been put to death. The loyal subjects of the Assembly had believed that this would please the Father. They had applauded, never once giving a single thought for the condemned men's souls.

These things hast thou done, and I kept silent. Thou thought I was like thee, yet I will reprove thee, and set them in order before thine eyes.

Gillean thought these words as he continued to gaze at the lifeless faces. These men had been decent and strong men, the type which the Assembly had wished to wipe from the earth, yet, for all their goodness, Gillean feared their souls may not have been secure. He knew that the Judge of all the earth would do right, yet the sadness of their loss continued to tear at his soul. It had a hold on him, and he could not let it go.

He remembered how their bodies had been left to hang. Strangely, they had not decayed as most would have. No bird nor animal had touched them, neither had time ravaged them. Though their souls had long departed, their mortal shells were somehow protected. Not until they had been cut down, had any part of them begun to decay.

The fact that he had found them here, still hanging, was a bitter thing. He wanted to speak to them, as the heathen sometimes spoke to their dead. Yet, knowing that they could not hear him, this desire was removed. Instead, he spoke to the Father, asking for comfort in this dark hour.

Gillean thought of his other good friend, Gordon Vordebt. He had been a brave man, one of the leaders of the Sons of Veritas. Gillean had long believed him to be dead, but he was not sure. He had vanished during a battle and had never been seen since. If he did live, he was far from here.

From behind him, a noise shook Gillean from his reverie. He stood up and whirled around, looked towards the sound. For a moment, his hand reached for his gun, but then he stopped. Standing in the trees not far off, was the soft and pale face of his late wife.

She stood so still, hardly seeming to breath, yet there was no evil in her eyes. They were as they once had been, warm and humble like dew of a summer morning. She looked at him and with her gaze, a flood of memories washed over him. They were not the bad memories, the fearful ones which had long haunted his dreams. They were the pleasant and joy-filled recollections of their life before, a beautiful time when they had been as close as flames of a fire.

A part of him understood that she was not real, yet, he could not convince his heart. He took a step towards her. She kept up her steady gaze, sad and methodical. There was pity there, but also a sense of regret. He wanted to desperately to comfort her, yet it was never to be. Another step and she began to fade. He called out to her, pleading with her to stay, but it was no use. In another breath she was gone, and nothing in this world could bring her back.

Gillean sat down again. He hung his head, caught somewhere between confusion and grief. His prayers returned as whispered sobs. He could not feel the Father's presence, yet he believed He was not far off. Gillean would wait here, continuing to pray till he heard from Him. Perhaps, as time passed, his mind might grow clearer. He could only hope.

As the afternoon passed into evening, Gillean kept still. He tried to refocus his mind, not wishing to dwell further on the past. At the moment, it seemed to hold only pain.

It was not much longer before he was approached by another visitor. Lifting his eyes, Gillean suddenly saw the woman with whom he had been corresponding: Amanda. She regarded him with her living blue eyes and gentle smile. She was just as fair, just as amazingly beautiful as she had been the last time he had seen her.

Gillean suddenly felt an overwhelming wave of guilt sweep over him. It felt wrong to look upon her, as if he had committed a sin. The wife of his youth was gone. She had left him, first through choice, then in death, yet he still felt as if he owed her something. Gillean felt torn in two. Amanda's spirit called out to him. In his heart he wanted to love her, yet a part of it rebelled against this notion. His spirit raged, a mixture of loss, hope, and sad confusion.

Amanda stepped back, yet did not turn away. Gillean looked back into her eyes and felt a sense of peace. It was as if she understood. His heart was calmed and so was his tremulous mind. It was as if she could read his thoughts, yet did not deem him crazy. This was a relief. Anyone else might, given his current mental state, bombarded by a jumble of thoughts and emotions he still struggled to control. Where had his inner discipline gone?

He smiled back at her, and she looked as if she might laugh. The light shimmered in her eyes and her golden har swayed in the wind, catching the slightest rays of the falling sun. When she spoke, the voice surprised him. It was sweet and feminine, yet with a stirring boldness.

"You haven't forgotten me." It was a statement, not a question. "You have not been forgotten of me. I still pray for you. Do you still pray for me?"

"I do. Every day. I've been meaning to write again. I hope to, it's just been so hard to find the time while traveling."

"I haven't been able to write. I've been ill. I've feared for my life. I think you may be ill, too."

He saw her gaze shift to his leg. Gillean looked down as well, and noticed a dark haze surrounding his right leg. The swelling seemed all but gone and it no longer hurt, yet the blackish vapor clung close, and followed, no matter how he turned it.

"What must I do?" He paused, considering how selfish he sounded. "What can I do for you."

"Continue to pray. Pray for my protection, and feverfew, I need feverfew."

"I will, I will. I think I can find some. I think they have some where I am. I'll..."

But she had gone. Amanda had departed as swiftly as she had come, fading into the shadowed trees.

For her, the dream had ended. Gillean would soon be waking up as well, yet even so, he would not escape strangeness. His nightmare was just beginning.

Chapter Nineteen:
Feverfew

Gillean opened his eyes. The threadbare curtains shrouding the window gleamed red bathing the room in a blood-tinged light. Head numb and spinning, he looked around the room. Mathias was gone. He had left silently while Gillean was still asleep, taking with him the short-barreled rifle which had once belonged to his master.

This surprised Gillean, yet he did not know why. They had spoken of parting ways once they reached the post. He was glad the man had sense enough not to go off without a weapon. He hoped Mathias would not be foolish enough to sell it, but realized this was probably the case. He would have to eat, and there was not much work here abouts.

Gillean gathered up his belongings. He strapped on his pack and tucked his pistols where they could be easily reached. His long coat concealed them well, along with the large knife he carried. Though many bore their weapons openly in places such as these, past experience had taught him to keep a low profile.

Once again, he inspected the contents of his saddle bags. He smiled, knowing they alone would be worth at least ten cans of beans. They contained several useful and high-value items: Bullets, matches, cloth scarves, a few old electronic devices with the circuit boards still intact, and even a small caliber pistol. The gun had a short, stubby barrel. It was the kind of weapon only effective when fired at pointblank range.

For a moment, Gillean wondered if the woman to whom it had belonged had ever used it to execute anyone. He quickly shoved the gun back in the bag and pushed the thought from his mind. Of course, she had. People like her were all the same. From what Mathias had told him, she had been maliciously wicked. She had not always been so, yet, her transformation had been unavoidable once the demons took hold. The change had not occurred over night, yet in the final stages of the transition, the monster within had risen swiftly and been most horrible to behold.

Gillean wondered what that must have felt like, for a human to rip away their better nature and throw it to the teeth of that which held them captive. Those creatures she kept, they had gained a savage hold on her, a hold which no mortal force could break. She had let them in, yet after that, they had become her masters. Like parasites, they had latched on to her soul, feeding every vile and sadistic thought, propelling, driving the darkest parts of her to rise. All the while, the beasts had continued eating up her inner heart. With ravenous, insatiable greed they had gobbled up all the light and empathy she had left.

    Gillean had experience with creatures such as these. Their hunger was truly limitless. Being not fully physical, they raged and lusted for the destruction of what was. Their deadliness lay in their willingness to put aside and postpone their appetite. These beasts flocked to men and women. Sensing their negative emotions, the bitterness and malice in their souls, they usually began by offering to do their dirty work for them. They would serve as assassins and false protectors, going after those the disgruntled people considered to be their enemies. That was when they made themselves indispensable. Gillean knew all too well, once they gained a claw-hold, their destructive powers would blossom. They would not remain content with domination of their "masters", their nature would not allow it. From the violence and conflicts they orchestrated, to the children snatched from their beds in the dark of night, their thirst and fever was the administration of death.

    Yet, no matter how blatant the cost, the altered, human hosts never seemed to understand what was happening, at least, not until the end. The cruel creatures always killed the humans with which they aligned themselves when they were ready to move on. They only ever had true allegiance to one: the man of darkness.

Toting his goods, Gillean proceeded down the creaking stairs. He passed the front desk,(he had paid for their supper and lodging the night before) and meandered out onto the sunken porch. It was almost as full as the bustling street.

More travelers and traders had arrived in the early hours. They jostled and haggled, milling about like flies in a bottle, a swarm of ragged degenerates. There seemed to be an increase in the general depravity of the place since his last visit. Vagabonds lay along the edges of the board-filled street, stoned out of their minds. On every dusty corner, prostitutes called and cackled loudly; some female, others more ambivalent in nature, all trying to rustle up some business.

Everyone looked drained and disheveled. Those who had been eating well nearly a year ago were now close to skin and bones. A great many of them appeared sick.

There was a time, not so very long ago, when Gillean would have been tempted reach out to these people. He would have wished to stand awhile in the dusty street and pray with the sick, perhaps witness to some of them and share from the Word of the Father. Doubtless, a great many of them needed prayer. Once or twice, he mumbled a blessing for some half-crazed woman, or bone-thin man, huddled against a pile of rubbish.

Apart from this, he kept his words and his beliefs to himself. He felt these people cared not for what he valued, neither had they the heart or will to understand. Subconsciously, Gillean knew his attitude was wrong, even possibly abhorrent in the eyes of his God. Still, he had his own concerns. There was much that needed doing this day, and he wished to avoid any excess trouble.

Had he but known what trouble was about to descend, Gillean might have felt and behaved differently. For some of these poor souls, this would be their final day. Yet, before the ending of their sad lives, they would be faced with a lie, a lie which would shackle them. Truth might have saved them and bared its wrongful root. Yet, for some, the deception was all but inevitable. Some hearts long for a lie, and the deceived know not that they are so.

After the ramshackle inn, Gillean's first transaction was to purchase a small cloth bag of feverfew. It was dried and beginning to crumble, yet this would not matter. It would still serve its purpose. Taking the vast majority of the brittle herb, he carefully placed it between the pages of the Father's word.

There was only a moment of questioning his own sanity then he continued down the street. Gillean gave the remainder of the herb to a coughing, old woman who showered him with blessings. He had considered keeping it, yet she looked as if she needed it more than he.

The little pistol from the evil woman brought a good price, as did the rest of his miscellaneous accoutrements. There was not the variety of canned goods and fresh fare which Gillean had hoped for. The supply of the stalls and stores were diminished. The scant crop in the northland had failed again. There were raiders combing the lands to the south, and the supply lines had been cut. Yet, in spite of these "temporary inconveniences", there was still some food. There were still some beans, rice, and other dried goods available.

Gillean loaded up on what supplies what foodstuffs he could obtain. He also bought bullets for the slide-bolt pistol and his revolver. Not surprisingly, their price had gone up, yet he paid it, trading the saddle bags, and some of his cash.

'Ere long, it was noon and the smelly streets had grown uncomfortably warm. Gillean knew he should be on his way, yet he still had some time before the dimming light of evening. After continuing to browse a bit more, he would leave Gaven post and make his way back towards the dried-up riverbed.

Well-rested, he intended to trek awhile past nightfall, making camp somewhere near the wreckage of the air-ships. Come morning, he might even look them over. Doubtless, they had all long ago been looted, yet it would do no harm. If he was careful and thorough, he might find some fuel which he could use as lighter fluid. In this world, there were few things which could not be repurposed.

As he neared the center of the trading post, he noticed a large crowd gathering in front of a building to his left. It had the look of an old church, and the gatherers appeared to be greatly enthused about the goings on inside.

Gillean did not want to stop, yet something in the buzz of the crowd made him curious. The hum of excitement drew him in, urging his unconscious need to know what was so important. He edged between the tight-knit bodies. The people, who noticed him, seemed alarmed at his presence here. They parted to admit him and looked at him with their wide, nervous gazes. Their eyes held the look of those belonging to wayward children, having been caught in the midst of some prohibited activity. Yet, in spite of their half-conscious guilt, they continued to press forward.

Gillean found himself caught up in their restless wave. He was propelled onward towards the wide and gaping doors of the church, for that was what it was. In another minute, he had been thrust through, into the dark and breathing jungle within.

Chapter Twenty:
The Strange Teacher

The interior of the aged chapel was dank and musty. The air stuck to his skin like the groping hands of the throng. As frightened dwellers from some dark cave, the men and women gasped and whispered. The hot air was stifling, stinking with the smell of breathing and unwashed bodies. It made Gillean uneasy. It felt like the makings of a deathtrap.

Taking a staggered breath, he flexed his shoulders and made to turn and leave; yet, before he could, a voice stayed him where he was. It was not harsh, or obviously evil, yet it held a fearful power, an icy strength which Gillean had seldom heard. Most disturbingly of all, the voice was not human. It was the sly, deep tone of a beast.

With reluctant eyes, Gillean turned towards the sound. The front of the sanctuary was more clearly lit. The walls were clean, painted in a shade of what should have been white, yet was now pale orange in the sputtering lamplight. The pulpit was black, a charred chunk of wood, perforated with holes and cracks, just as the walls in the inn had been.

It took Gillean a moment to realize what he was looking at. The creature was perched atop the pulpit. The thing was half the size of a man and covered in a coat of short, reddish brown fur. The beast's tiny black eyes peered out from its narrow head, seeming to twinkle as it glanced around the room. Its long, rounded snout drooped, then twitched as it smelled the air. It shifted its weight, then pawed at the air. When the creature spoke again, its words stung like a needle in Gillean's mind.

"Hear me now, followers in the ranks of enlightenment. You need no remission of your sins. As you gain understanding, you shall be endowed with the knowledge that the concept of sin is just another lie. It is a fabricated idea meant to shun you into reverting to what has failed you, vain religion which you do not require. Ye must save yourselves. You say you look for God to return. Tell me, have ye seen him? I have. God lives inside of you. Accept this truth and ye shall never walk alone. Ye shall walk as the gods ye are."

Those listening seemed pricked in their hearts. They were entranced, seemingly entrapped by the words of the beast. To Gillean, the creature was ugly, yet to everyone else, he was beautiful, a creature of light and grace.

"Yes," said the beast, "I speak the truth. Ye are all gods. So it says in the Word and so it is. Trust your hearts for these are the homes of the gods. Ye must feed them, grow them up strong unto the edification of thy wills. Learn to listen to the many gods inside of you. Give unto them life that they might live, and in turn, give back to thee."

"Oh, most noble beast!" a voice shot up from the crowd, "how shall we accomplish this? How shall we do it, and when it is done, know that it was done well?"

A murmur of agreement rose from the clustered masses. The speaker had a valid point. How would they know? The many mumblings fell silent in anticipation of the speaking beast's response.

"You shall know. You shall know, for there is one who shall show you; a greater spirit, a god more powerful than any which has ever been conceived or imagined."

The creature continued. "Behold, I tell you a mystery. He is four, and these four are one, one who comes to devastate his enemies, the enemies of creation. It is he who shall show ye the way of the divine. He shall bring you into union with all life. Answer me if you can, who is like unto the beast, that terror embodied in four? Who can make war against him? Who shall challenge him? Take heed, all you who would be saved, and understand. His servants are already at work in this great land. If you shall harken, he shall come to you with mercy in his wings. Yet, if you should anger him, if you should blaspheme this great and glorious king; he shall send his arms-man, the one with yellow eyes, to punish you. Do not be as fools. Submit yourselves unto him while there is yet time. Submit yourselves and pray unto the spirit of the four."

The shivering people hummed and bletted in approval. They began to sway, rocking back and forth, making and ancient foundations shift with their weight. If they had not been entranced before, they surely were now. The spell of the demonic creature had become absolute.

From the moment he had heard the thing begin to speak, Gillean had endeavored to steel his mind. All throughout the bizarre monologue, his spirit had been calling out to the Father for protection. He had not heard any warning from the still, small voice; yet now, he felt it in his soul. It was crying out, not necessarily calling for him to leave, yet feverishly, ardently reviling the words of the red-furred prophet.

Believing he had heard enough of this weirdness, Gillean decided that it was time to go. He started to turn around, yet, found he could not. His limbs and muscles seemed frozen in place. A sense of sheer, heart-pounding panic rushed through him. He heard the people groaning, their faces bleached and lifeless like those of scarecrow zombies. The pit-like eyes of the creature looked as if they could swallow up the room. They bored into Gillean, their lidless gaze hovering like death itself.

Gillean's leg throbbed. He could feel the poison moving again, coursing and cutting through his veins. It meant to paralyze his heart.

Gillean might have remained like this for some time, had not events taken another, wholly unexpected turn.

From across the room, there was an explosion of white-hot lightning. It tore between the entranced individuals and struck the pulpit with a blinding flash. Dust and splinters of broken wood. The tamandua, (for that was what the creature was) tumbled off its perch and hit the floor. With a cry much like that of a dying rabbit, it leapt up and bolted, followed by several more of the wood-shattering explosions.

The spell broken, Gillean turned unhindered to try and ascertain the source of the blasts. To his left, the crowed had stumbled back to reveal none other than Mathias. He stood in the waning light, feet apart, holding his rifle. He had tried to kill the creature for its lies. His aim had been off, still, Gillean was impressed. The man had done fairly well, considering his lack of training and experience with firearms. There was a certain pride in his stalwart stance. Not the vain and foolish pride which topples kingdoms, but the honorable pride of one who stands for what is right.

Once they had recovered from their sudden shock, the people began to flee. They raced from the dim-lit sanctuary with cries of terror upon their lips. It was as if they had just witnessed a murder. The only ones who did not run were Gillean and Mathias.

Gillean regarded the screaming masses with something between pity and bemusement. A moment ago, they had been ready and willing to pledge their immortal souls to that red furball and his mystic quartet god. Now, they seemed like animals themselves, scattering and running over each other as if they had lost their minds.

No one had risen up to challenge Mathias, not yet. All the same, Gillean felt they should be making themselves scarce. As the last wailing "seekers of truth" sprinted out the door, he stepped over to his friend and attempted to get his attention.

Chapter Twenty-one:
Hemmed In

"Good shooting pastor. You did what needed to be done. The rascal got away, but he'll meet his destruction in the end. Let us go. Let us leave this den of darkness before that crowd comes to their senses. They might not be happy you wrecked their prayer meeting."

Mathias started at the sound of Gillean's voice. He turned violently, as if ready to fight, yet calmed when he saw who it was. His eyes were wide and his forehead covered in sweat. He clung to the gun with shaky hands. If they had been this way before, Gillean noted, he never would have been able to hit so close to his mark. The Spirit of the Father was known to give courage as needed.

"You're right. We should go. I, I did not want to shoot. I just couldn't let that creature continue speaking. I, I heard the devil in him."

"Yes," said Gillean, "And so he was. That accursed creature was full of the devil and all which lives at enmity with God. You did right, but now we must go."

The two of them rushed for the back of the creaking church, in the direction which the varmint had scampered. There were several smaller rooms and a coat closet, yet there was no back door, there was not even a single window. Beginning to feel nervous again, Gillean and Mathias crept back through the sanctuary and towards the front entrance. They were stopped short however, by the formerly frightened crowd which had closed in to bar their way.

The faces of the worshipers were dark, their eyes burning like coals of poisoned fire. They were silent and dreadful, inspiring that feeling which comes when you strike a nest of hornets. Most appeared to be unarmed, yet a few held knives, and Gillean could see the prominent shape of several scatter-gun barrels rising from their midst.

As they stood at stalemate, a low chant began to rise up from the outer edges. As it worked its way through the throng, it grew louder and increasingly more pronounced. "Bigot! Bigot!" they cawed, waving their fists and brandishing their rusty knives.

Gillean had heard this word used before, yet was not sure he could remember its meaning. Mathias knew exactly what it meant. This was not his first run-in with an angry mob, one of the setbacks of being an aspiring pastor in a world that has gone to ruin.

Gillean did not like their odds. There was no clear path of escape. He had fought his way out of messes like this before, yet it would be a true wonder if they made it through this one unscathed. They were hemmed in.

They might be able to hold the door, gunning down whoever tried to rush through, yet they would be forced pull back eventually. They had not enough bullets for half this number and the hostile mob was growing even now. Soon, other guns would be joining this fight.

Still, Gillean was determined to make a stand and die on his feet. His slide-bolt pistol was in his hand, a round chambered and waiting. His other hand rested on the grip of his double action revolver. As always, the shedding of human blood was distasteful to him, yet, he was no stranger to war. Besides, these fools had had their chance.

A big, burly woman with bug eyes and a meat-cleaver was edging towards them. She was getting to close for comfort. Gillean was all ready to end her when Mathias touched his shoulder. At the same time, Gillean listened and could hear that unmistakable whisper, the communication of the still, small voice. It calmed his soul and without another thought, he lowered his gun.

"Follow me," Mathias said. He stepped forward towards the seething crowd.

For one terrible instant, Gillean feared that they would grab him and tear him to bits, yet nothing happened. Mathias moved between the men and women as if they had not seen him. Dazed and a trifle confused, Gillean followed suit.

They had been delivered once again. Their lives had been saved, and they had found favor in the eyes of the Father. This was truly cause for thanksgiving.

Unfortunately, they were not, as some old folk would say, "out of the woods yet."

Just as they cleared the tangled, yelling throng, there came a thunderous noise from above. As if out of nowhere, there was a storm of dust and debris and the largest air-ship Gillean had ever seen was roaring down on them. The forces of the Assembly had arrived.

Chapter Twenty-two:
Owl Head

The ground began to shake. The boardwalks and rugged buildings swayed as if they would fall, then danced a jig. They rattled and convulsed as the vibrations from the giant craft racked the earth and air.

People were screaming, scattering, tumbling over each other in a panicked scramble. Some fell flat on their faces screaming out prayers to whatever god they esteemed. They cowered in the shadow of what loomed above.

The monolithic object blotted out the sky. As it descended, plumes of white steam billowed from its undercarriage. At the center of its base was the insignia of the Assembly: that hated scarlet A rimmed above and below by laurels. It looked for all the world like a glaring eye, regarding disdainfully those it would soon punish. Gillean remembered that symbol well from his time in the prison camps. The thought of the thousands who had suffered and died beneath its "sacred" gaze made his blood boil. He had hoped that these fascistic rulers, these stealers of children and slayers of the old, would die out with the rest of this blighted world, yet this did not seem to have been the case. He should have known. Their kind would always endure. As long as there were those desiring subjugation in exchange for safety, the cowardly and the weak-minded; as long as men and women chose the power of a lie over the conviction of truth, tyranny would triumph.

Pulling Mathias with him, Gillean ducked into a dingey store-front. They hunkered down behind the front window, waiting for what would come next. They both knew better than to run. At this point, that would prove fruitless.

Sure enough, from the edge of the post, there came the sickening pulse of gunfire. The Assembly forces had surrounded this place and had cut off those attempting to escape. Whatever their business, the aggressors required all those present to remain. It was not long before a flow of disheartened folk began to join those cowering in the street. They were goaded forward by tall men in black armor carrying small, box-like guns. The faces of the shepherds were obscured by dark masks devoid of eyes. They moved like machines, menacing the people and ordering them to huddle where the street widened. Gillean noted with increasing unease that some of their voices seemed mildly inhuman. He shuddered as a chill crept into his bones. From across the way, he thought he could see the shimmer of stale candlelight. This was not good.

Before them, the gargantuan craft was landing. It eased down slowly over four of the buildings, crushing them flat. A shower of glass and splinters popped and scattered as it lurched, finally coming to rest.

There was a rush of air and a malicious hissing. One of the great, portside doors slid open, wreathed by smoke. From within, there was a clanking; then the he appeared.

The man was tall, clad in black armor like the others, only his was tighter, more slimly fitted to reveal his muscular shape. This was partially covered by a long, dark trench coat which hung from his massive shoulders like a shroud.

He was a giant, towering at least seven feet in height. Upon his head, he wore what looked like an old metal helmet of the type knights in fairy tales used to wear. It was dented and rusty, having one solitary slit for the eyes and no other opening. It was an oddity, a strange thing for a soldier of the Assembly to wear. On anyone else, it might have seemed comically out of place. Yet there was nothing amusing about this dark one. He held no weapon in his hands, yet, from the feeling radiated by his dreadful personage, he might not have needed one. Gillean sensed that this man had hundreds, if not thousands of guns at his command. All he would have to do was snap his fingers and the entirety of Gaven post would be turned into swiss cheese. Yet, he was not just a man. This fellow was something more, something hideously evil. An apparition born of nightmares.

As he stood and surveyed the frightened crowds, the man's head seemed to move apart from his body. His massive shoulders budged and swelled, as if struggling to contain some hidden strength. For one dreadful moment, Gillean thought the black slit of the helmet was peering directly at them.

As the steam continued to roll off the metal sides of the air-ship, the commander spoke.

"People of the post, ill-fated guests. How come you this day to be so out of countenance? What trouble has beset your minds? Rejoice, for this day is thy calling established. The Sacred Assembly has need of your services."

The man paused as if to clear his throat, yet nothing emerged from the helmet but a muffled, inhuman gargle.

"You have no water here. All your wells have run dry. The proprietors of this place have hoarded what they can. They have tried to conceal this fact from you, yet the truth was soon to be discovered."

He gave what must have been a laugh. It sounded grating and strangely high-pitched for a man, almost like a reedy chortle.

"You have nowhere to turn. You will never make it out of this wasted desert. The deadlands are as dry as the bones of your fathers and the great moor has no moisture to offer. The spring at its southeastern edge had been polluted. You have but one choice, one option before you. Join our ranks. We have plenty of water. Play a part in the rebuilding of our world and you shall be richly rewarded. I myself shall see to it."

There was a pause. In the stillness, the only sound was the wind and the slow humming pulse of the great machine as it continued to sweat and steam. Suddenly, a voice cried out.

"How do we know you speak the truth? Why should we trust you? Why should we trust the Assembly? What have you ever brought us but pain and death?"

There was a gasp of shock, then a slow faint murmur of agreement. This did not last, however. The speaker's comrades quickly fell silent under the chilling gaze of the helmet.

As if on cue, the crowd parted to reviled the man who had spoken. He was a lanky fellow, middle-aged and dressed in faded denim, a knit cap resting crookedly on his head. Though he had seemed brave surrounded by his cohorts, he was not so now. As he realized he stood alone, all the color drained from his face. His lips began to move and it looked to Gillean as if he was praying. Gillean hoped it was to the Father. No one else could help him now.

The tall man did not answer in words only in action. With one smooth movement he brushed back the trench coat and drew out a pistol. The death-black barrel convulsed as the shot burst forth. It slammed into the questioner sending him sprawling before anyone had a chance to react. In the searing echo, the man lay dead and the dark commander continued to stand tall.

Barely moving, he replaced the gun and let forth another shrill, threaded cackle. Gillean saw the man's hands move to the helmet, and a horrible shiver passed through his soul. He did not want to see what was beneath it, yet he was unable to look away. He heard the hiss of Mathias's breath and knew he faced the same paradoxical dilemma.

Slowly, the dented helmet was lifted off, and all who gazed upon the stranger knew true terror. The first thing they saw were his eyes, his enormous, yellow eyes, the pupils of which burned black like living death. There was no nose or mouth, only a cruelly hooked silver beak. The man's head was that of an owl, a great and hideous owl with bristling gray-white feathers. The tufts above his eyes curled out like knit brows, and as he looked at them, they knew, to refuse his directions was to invite death.

One by one, the other soldiers removed their masks. Wolf, cat, rabbit, goat: the eyes of each glared with similar intensity, a kindred spirit of sadistic hate. These were mavarians, or something like them. Gillean had not sensed that musty smell which usually proceeded them, yet this did not matter. They were here now and these poor people were doomed.

"So, what then shall it be?" the owl man croaked. "The Assembly is in need of servants, yet also slaves. The choice is yours, yet be ye warned. This poor degenerate died swiftly. Your end shall not be so if ye cross us. There be water, yet only for those who open their hearts. The rest of ye shall slake your thirst with blood."

Chapter Twenty-three:
The Fall

Amanda has been fighting for her life. Inside the strange and shadowy room, the fire is always burning. The flames are never fed, yet they never died. In her fever, she would wake, day after day, night after night, always to the burning light of the enormous hearth.

The room was hot, hotter than a cloudless summer, but dark. The continual flames did not give off much light. Sweat poured from her skin, but not always. Other times she was cold, so cold, that Amanda felt as if she might freeze to death even in this boiling room. The covers on the bed were her shelter, then an hour later, her suffocation. She would fling them off of her, struggling to breath; then she found herself reaching for them, trying to pull them back, to recapture some of the warmth which had plagued her only moments before. Her body was racked, twisted and punished by the assault of everchanging extremes. They may have only been perceived, yet to Amanda, they were real, and they were killing her slowly.

This illness, this fever, it had been caused by more than just exposure to damp and cold. She had realized this ever since the terrifying dream. She had more dreams, yet none of them were clear.

Everything was wreathed in shadows, distorted by that strange and undying fire which shared the room.

In both sleeping and waking, her prayers were constant. Though she was tormented, she never lost sight of the one remaining truth. No matter what befell her, regardless of her life or death, God loved her and He would remain with her through it all. He was not some far off distant stranger, some mystic spirit robed in obscurity; neither was he a hesitant gentleman waiting for some unconscious rendering of her will. He was a father; a tender, caring, ever-present father who would not depart no matter how dark the night or steep the path. By His good grace she clung to life, even through her agony and sorrow.

There were times, as in her olden days, when Amanda wanted to give in. A part of her wanted to die, to close her eyes and let go of her spirit. Yet, the still, small voice sustained her: for life, though seared by suffering, is still life, and where it continues there is hope. When the Father gives a gift, none can take it away save for He himself who gave it, and He gave to her life. It came to her in the most bitter moment of her darkest night. Its touch and savor were a wave of wonderous awe, like crystal-clear water washing a dry and weary land. It was living water, so cool and sweet, welling up within her to replenish what was drained away. It fed not only her physical body but her soul. And above it all, the joyous, heart-felt song: the beautiful voice of the Father, singing over her.

Opening her eyes again, Amanda struggled to sit up. With tremulous hands, she reached for the Word of the Father. She knew not how it had followed her here. The morning of the day Hector had moved her, she had left it in its accustomed hiding place. He had not brought it to her room, for he could not touch it, of this much she was sure. The aged tome lay atop the mahogany table beside her bed. It called to her softly as if had many a time before. Though its faded cover and binding were of black leather, it held a golden glow, endowed with radiant anointing from another realm on high.

Reaching out, Amanda took hold of the book. She pulled it to chest, embracing it, then opening it to view its truth. At first, the words were blurred, partially because of her spinning head, and in part due to the sweat which stung her eyes. For a moment, Amanda feared she would not be able to read, yet with prayer, the holy writing became clear.

Though the still, small voice had proved a comfort, she needed the reassurance of the Word. Its truth had been her help, had calmed her so many times before. Yet, as she delved through the pages, she felt dismay begin to take hold. Where once she had found peace and enlightenment, now it spoke of only death and desolation.

Once again, Amanda prayed, and again she searched, only to find more of the same. The pleasant scriptures seemed lost to her. She knew they were there, the Word of the Father never changed. Yet they were somehow hidden, and all she could view were those pertaining to judgement and the ending of life. It was a discovery both shocking and bitter.

Continuing to turn the brittle leaves, she endeavored to open her heart and listen for God's voice. Some small thread of guidance or encouragement was all she needed, some word of affection from above. There was only silence, and the glow of laughing flames, their shadows seemingly more ghoulish than ever. Were they the flames of Hell? Was this a sign, a manifestation of her new and terrible fate? How swiftly had she forgotten the Father's love for her, His gentle singing. In His silence, her fears and doubts threatened to drive her to derision. The fever was beginning to weaken her again. Inside, there was a dreadful sinking feeling, as if a plug had been pulled and all the life was draining out of her.

No, this could not be. The Father's words and promises were faithful and true. He was not like mortal man. There was no shadow of turning with him. Yet, why then did she suddenly feel so afraid, like an orphan child cast out to die in the cold of a moonless night? Why was God so dreadfully silent? Had she been deceived concerning his love for her? Had she been deceiving herself all along? Perhaps she was not thinking rationally. Perhaps this sickness had affected her mind. Then again, she had placed words in the mouth of her Lord before, many times unwittingly, yet she had done it. Had she done so here, unknowingly motivated by foolish hopefulness and desire? Was this her punishment for such an offense, her true and bitter fate?

Amanda could hear Hector's words within the rasp and crackle of the hungry flames. "Your precious God and Father has forgotten you. He has cut you off and utterly shut you out. This is your just consequence, your reward for betrayal and mariticide."

She rebuked them even as they fell upon her ears, yet they cut her all the same. She had grieved night and day for ages since the death of her husband. She had repented of the part she had played in his demise, had begged God ceaselessly for forgiveness. She had hoped she had been forgiven, yet her faith on this score had long been weak indeed. In truth, a part of her had never quite forgiven herself.

She had betrayed him to save her family, her cold, inconsiderate, spiteful step-parents and their arrogant children. They had never valued her, never treated her as one of their own. Their care of her, if it could have been called that, was more out of obligation than true affection. They had not loved her, and despite her long-held desire to please them, they had spit upon her sacrifice, repaying it with brutal beatings and all manner of vile abuse.

The one person who had cared for her, who had valued her as she was, was dead and gone. She had watched from a high window as his head had been severed from his body. That last look in his warm, beautiful eyes would haunt her forever, as would his final words.

"All I have done was for you. I love you my darling, Farewell."

The seeds of doubt and depression continued to work their way within her burdened mind. She struggled against them, attempting to cast them out even as the cursed fever spiked and a new wave of convulsions racked her feeble form.

With tears and shuddered gasps, Amanda frantically combed through the pages of the Father's Words, searching for something to renew her hope. It seemed ages since she had heard from Gillean, that caring stranger who had befriended her from so great a distance. As far as she was aware, he had never responded to her plea for feverfew. She knew not whether this was because he had none, or whether he had forgotten about her.

That would make sense, she thought. *Everyone else has forgotten, and why should they not.*

There was a sudden numbness in her chest. The writhing strands of fire wavered and waned. Their light receded as if they might soon die. Their warmth was gone, stolen away by some unseen pall. The temperature was dropping steadily. The chill caught in her lungs, making her cough, causing sparks of pain to flash before her eyes.

From somewhere above, the sound of dread, the beating of wings. They drummed with fervent malice just as they had from the roof of her hovel. Then came the scratch and scrape of talons, followed by the low, deep call of an owl.

There was a moment when she wanted to give up. Wearied and disheartened by her plight, Amanda was frightened and sick within her soul. She had given all she had in the struggle to resist the lies. She was tired of fighting. This lonely war seemed to have no end, no conclusion in sight. How much simpler would it be to just shut down. She could close her eyes and breath out, resolving never to fill her lungs again. She would release her hold on life, and with it, this agony which so easily beset her. She would drift, she would sink unconscious into that black, unfathomable void. It was all around her now, and its presence was growing, ebbing up like pitch-black waves from the places which the shadows touched. It called so sweetly in the wake of bitter pain.

"Let this end," It seemed to say. *"Let it end. Give in to the nothing and rest in peace."*

The voice was soothing, poignant in its prick. It made so much sense and gave so little fear.

But no, she had been given a promise, the most sacred promise ever spoken; the pledge that life would outstrip death, that light would endure past the time of darkness. She would not throw away such a hope as this, not lightly.

Striking back her doubts and claiming what little strength remained, Amanda pulled herself from the sticky sheets and attempted to stand. The weight and press of gravity beat down on her, and her own feet and legs seemed loath to obey. Yet, still she moved, like one who has arisen from the dead, slowly, tentatively, till she had found her footing. Somehow, she kept her balance.

The weary maiden felt her heart rise and fall with every breath. For a moment, the flames seemed to flare and call to her, yet faded as she turned from them. Looking past the reach of their wavering light, she saw the door. It stood tall and stone-like, without latch or knob.

With no other thought than to escape this prison, she threw herself against it, and miraculously, it gave way to the weight of her body. She stumbled yet did not fall. She wandered out into a crisp autumn night, lit by a full and radiant moon. It was then that her fever began to break.

Her illness was still with her, yet, its symptoms had abated. The pain and ache seemed distant and suppressed, restrained by the fresh and open air. Amanda breathed it in gratefully. Looking up to the star-strewn sky, she whispered a prayer of thanksgiving and a humble request of guidance.

She could see to dark forest and the quarry where she had worked, its gray cliffs now white in the moon-light. The nightgown she wore was thin, yet she did not feel a chill. There was a stirring, a gathering within her blood. This was the hour of her escape. Tonight, at last she would be free.

As if in delayed answer to her prior pleas, Amanda found herself endowed with new strength. Her heart began to pump and her breathing became smooth and even, in spite of the cold. It flowed like the wind, becoming almost effortless with her movements. Its cool touch swelled within her, making her almost giddy, compelling her to run; and run she did, leaving thought and fear behind her.

The forest path raced beneath her bare feet. The pine boughs waved then rushed away, followed by beech and alder. She had never made it this far before. In the past, any who dared venture half this distance would have long ago been felled by the enchantment. It seemed to have lost its hold on her.

So pleased was she with her new found liberty that Amanda failed to realize she had left the path. Suddenly, she lost her footing and fell. She braced herself, expecting to feel the impact of the forest floor, yet it never came.

In a moment of sheer horror and disbelief, Amanda was swallowed up by a deeper darkness. She continued to fall, spinning and tumbling down the black throat of an ancient well. It had lain in the center of her unconsciously chosen path, abandoned and concealed for centuries. It had been dug by a people long forgotten with tools long passed from knowledge. The makers of this deep abyss had used pipes to draw from the aquifer far beneath, yet those were now gone. All that remained was the pit, the pit of unfathomable depths into which Amanda now plummeted.

As she fell, a single scripture arose to haunt her panicked mind. It seemed a paradox, yet she knew with certainty that it was true.

"Thou fool, that which thou sowest is not quickened, except it die."

This was her last thought as she descended past the stony walls. Long before she reached the bottom, her consciousness departed her. She never felt the impact.

Chapter Twenty-four:
Leaving

Mathias and Gillean did not even have to speak. They both knew that it was time to depart. Surrounded or no, Gaven post had become a doomed town; and they would most certainly be caught it they remained. They could hide and pray to be passed over, yet the gray Mavarians would surely smell them out. They had a knack for that kind of thing. Being the rumored spawn of demons, it was believed that they possessed a kind of sixth sense. It was a struggle to hide one's thought from them, especially fear and grief. They had a way of getting inside your head and using your emotions against you. Calling upon the Father helped, as well as invoking the protection of His Spirit, yet the only sure way was to flee from them. It was true they could be killed, or disembodied; as the case may be, yet even then, even when their skin had turned to ash and crumbled away, their presence could still pursue you.

Keeping low, the two men moved past rows of rickety, disheveled shelves. Reaching the back of the store, they heard the screaming and cries of dismay from the street. Apparently, the brutality of the ghoulish mutants was just getting started.

If Gillean's past experiences were any indication of what was to unfold, most likely the entire trading post would be taken, with the exception of those slain for example, or just out of pure sadistic evil. The forces of the Assembly would kill whoever resisted. Life was not precious to them. They would then ransack the market and all the stores, seizing anything and everything of value. These "people" were known for being thorough.

As they crept through a dark room filled with broken crates, Gillean recalled an old song from the days of his youth. They had been blessed with more music back then, and something the old people had called "radio". It felt like an age since the last of those airwaves had gone dead. The song itself had not been popular, yet its lyrics had lingered with him all the same.

"When things which should not speak tell lies,
    And hidden are our once fair skies,
    Then even so, Lord, quickly come,
    Before all men are made as dumb."

The words seemed to sink inside his mind, as if permeating some deeper level which had long ago been locked away. The song hadn't made much sense to him back then, yet now, in light of what they were living, its meaning seemed perfectly clear.

Gillean thought of how there had been a general lack of communication between the members of the crowd. They had pulled together to threaten them outside the church, yet they had not made eye contact with each other, even before things became chaotic. Their chants and mutterings, though in unison, had in fact seemed somehow disconnected. They had stood together, yet alone, like a flock of disoriented gulls. Each one would follow the example of the others, yet none truly cared for the wellbeing of his neighbor. It had been like staring down a herd of mad cattle. Gillean wondered, if the owl man had not shown up, how long it would have taken for these people to have become completely stupid.

As they pushed and fought their way to what they hoped was a back door, a cacophony of noise split their eardrums. The sounds of erupting gunfire shook all that was. The front widow burst with a jingling crash, and bullets tore past them, punching gleaming holes in the dirt-brown walls.

From the rooftops, men and women were yelling, their cries shrill, their choked voices caught somewhere between despair and reckless rage. Gillean decided the inhabitants and visitors of the post must have weighed their options and had chosen death in lieu of servitude. Having himself been a prisoner of the Assembly, he could hardly blame them; besides, these invaders were

Mavarians. Creatures such as these could never be trusted to keep their word. They were the standard bearers of perdition and the children of the father of lies.

"For the children!" he heard an old woman scream. "Kill em all! For the children!"

Of course, there had not been any children in these parts for some time. Gillean assumed she was referring to all those which had been taken nigh on seven years ago, abducted by the Assembly for their own obscene ends. He realized that there were still plenty of disgruntled parents left alive, and they would do whatever they could to strike back at those who had robbed them of their young.

"The thief came not but to kill, steal, and destroy," Gillean muttered under his breath as he kicked the backdoor. It fell apart like rotten siding, leaving a cloud of fetid, moldering dust in its wake.

Glancing about hurridly, weapons raised and at the ready, the two of them ran down a narrow alleyway. They moved like ghosts, Gillean quickly plotting the safest way forward and Mathias following. Though they were moving through the alleys at a rapid pace, he could tell the older man was looking for something; some device or machine to assist them in their escape.

Behind one of the old buildings on the edge of town, they found what they needed. It was an old vehicle. The kind powered by the black fuel. It was large, with massive, thick-treaded tires and a grill crafted to look like the open jaws of some savage beast. It was open topped with long metal bars running the length of the body and some sort of shield fitted to the rear end. Mathias had his doubts. He had never seen a contraption quite like this, much less ridden in one. He had heard his share of stories, everyone had, yet to consider actually getting into one and speeding away... The whole concept seemed incredibly unsafe.

As if sensing his thoughts, Gillean glared at him and growled. "Listen, pastor, we don't have time to debate this or find another option so climb on in. They are going to be shooting at us, but don't worry, these things are fast. Just keep your head down and pray it runs smooth."

"So, you've driven one of these things before?" Mathias asked hesitantly as he climbed inside.

"Yes," Gillean said matter of factly, "I have. It's been about four of five years, but all the stuff is pretty much the same...I think. Let's just do this. Look in the back, see if there's any weapons stashed here. I'll ger her started."

"Isn't this stealing?"

"No, not really. I don't think the previous owners will be needing it. Something tells me the Assembly won't be taking any prisoners this raid."

Mathias settled into one of the rear-facing seats. There was a large and bulky tarp directly behind him, but rather than investigate what lay beneath, he decided to first strap himself in. This was a wise choice, for no sooner had he done so, that a dark form appeared at the front of an adjacent alley. Mathias cried a warning, but Gillean had already seen him.

In a burst of putrid smoke, the engine roared to life; and they were off, racing between the crooked structures like a dog with its tale on fire. There was a screaching cry, and Mathias saw a man with an owl's head, much like that of the commander. Mathias shot him in the chest, but not before the monster placed a hand upon his neck setting off some kind of alarm. Suddenly, the air resounded with the sound of wailing sirens.

Gillean gunned the engine and they hurtled away. They sped between the last few buildings at breakneck speed, racing out across the dead lands in a cloud of dust. They were headed west, but turning north. Far off in the distance, dark peaks shimmered in the fading light. If they could reach them by nightfall, they could take refuge in the caves which lined their slopes. They would have to abandon their vehicle, but that was all right. He doubted it would even have enough fuel to span the distance, yet they had to try. They would have enough to keep them rolling until nightfall. After that, they could ditch the machine any time. He doubted the enemy would pursue them very far, and if they did, they most likely would not use many airships and none of the big ones. For now, their focus was the loot and rape of Gaven post. He prayed that was where their focus would remain.

They were really starting to cover some ground. Gillean's motorist skills were beginning to return to him. This was good. They still had their food and their weapons, as well as whatever was under the tarp, and so far, there were no signs of pursuit. Just then, Mathias let loose what sounded like a stifled shriek. Fighting the urge to speak obscenities, Gillean looked over his shoulder to see two armored air-ships and five small ground craft headed out after them.

Asking forgiveness for what he had almost blurted out, Gillean prayed to his Lord. They would not be getting out of this one without help, that was certain. As fast as this thing could take them, the Assembly's crafts were faster. Soon, they would be right on their tail, and those heavy guns were some of the best and most accurate ever made.

"Mathias! Brace yourself. How many shots do you have left in the rifle?"

"I don't know! One, I think!"

He could hardly hear over the roar and thrum of the engine, yet he was sure he could hear Gillean gritting his teeth.

"Okay! Here!" Gillean held out his slide-bold pistol. "Whatever you do, do not lose this! Don't start shooting till you can see the faces of those riding up on us! On the air ships, aim for the turbines and the center glass of the cockpits! On the ground vehicles aim center mass at the drivers! Make every shot count! I'll do what I can from up here! Hang on! It's gonna get rough!"

Chapter Twenty-five:
A New Name

Coldness, and the feeling of being forgotten; these were the sensations to which Amanda slowly woke. She was sinking. All around her, the dark and glacial waters hung motionless. There was no current.

Somewhere far above, there was the gleam of light and the promise of air. They called to her, yet were far beyond her reach. They were like ghosts; the remnants of a treasured memory, something longed for which may never live again.

She knew she had to breathe. She must fill her lungs with air, or die. The realization remained with her; yet, for some strange reason, it did not seem important to act on it. Her lungs felt light, unburdened. There was no pressure stabbing against them, no panicked urge to let loose a soundless scream and allow the water to come rushing in.

Amanda felt as if she could remain here, content to let the numbing depths draw here where they would. Soon, nothing would matter. Blackness would wash clear her mind and lull her into rest. Surely, all her failings had been forgiven. What reason was there to fight?

There was not much thought left to her in that dark and dream-like place. What memories she had seemed scattered and surreal. None of them seemed overly important or worth harboring for long. She was far removed, cast away from all she had known. Her former worlds were as transient dreams passed on without regard. And this: this was sweet and peaceful death, come at last to take her home. She wanted to see those waiting for her on the other side. Her long-lost companions and that one whom she had wronged so deeply. She knew he would be there and that he had forgiven her.

Amanda could hear the voices of the angels calling to her in wistful, poignant tones. "Come and walk with us," they said. "Come and walk with us in the garden. See the flowers and how they shine: the roses, how red; the lilies, how wonderfully white. Look here, a special blossom, just for you."

In her mind's eyes, she could see. The bloom glowed with a radiance soft and simple, like the sheen of a harvest moon. Its petals were heart-shaped, pure white laced with lavender and pink. Its aroma was equally wondrous. It was like honey and the earthy dew of a summer's morn. Even in her early years, Amanda had never seen anything like it in her world.

Along with the lovely image, she hears a name. It is the name of the flower. It is called Ameara. Amanda likes this name. It appeals to her. It clings unto her soul, reminding her of a time when there was true sunlight and a world growing and breathing with life.

The flower appeared so clear and vibrant in its wild beauty, she believed it was blooming directly before her. With tentative hands, she reached out to touch it. She wanted to take it up and hold it close as her life ended.

In a sudden spark of pain, the image fled away. In her head there was a ripping sound, like the tearing of thick paper. The need to breath hit her like a storm of ice and needles. Her lungs were screaming. They were red hot, burning as if about to literally combust. She must rise, she has no choice. Amanda tries to swim upward, but she cannot. Something is holding her down.

Suddenly, she realizes she is being crushed, not by the pressure of the water, but by an enormous snake which had wrapped itself about her. Its coils constrict again, closing upon her tender waist and the delicate tissue of her neck.

Now comes the moment of panick, that instant of sheer horrified struggle. Now Amanda realizes the truth. She wants to live on. She wants it desperately. The strength of terrified fear courses through her limbs and attacks her heart like a jackhammer.

Kicking herself up through the swirling abyss of liquid gloom, she claws at her captor, striking at him again and again. The scaly hide is thick, yet she digs her nails into it, gouging at the tensing muscles. The coils only pull tighter. It's a losing battle and she knows it. Yet still, that feverish fire, that last burst of defiance before then end, keeps her fighting a moment more.

For one terrifying instant, she can see the thing's massive head as it turns to look at her. Two pricks of translucent light stare back at her from the gloom. They are cold, slitted, and sinister, maliciously anticipating her demise.

Suffocation seems imminent now. The serpent is too strong and she is too weak. They are both too far from the surface and her strength is about to fold.

As blackness encircled her sight, Amanda cried out in her heart. She did not have time for words, only a silent yearning plea of the spirit.

Now, it was the weighted depths which seemed as a dream. The snake's hold had all but wrung the life from her bones; and they were sinking, sinking further and further from the light, falling from time and consciousness. Everything was shutting down. The darkness was an endless shroud. She could feel nothing.

Suddenly, with a fierceness rivaling the once brilliant-sun, the light roared over her. From somewhere above, a great and mighty voice boomed out, like thunder over the mountains.

"SHE SHALL LIVE!"

The coils of the serpent fell away. It was gone and she was sailing upward towards the source of the diving light. She felt like she was flying on the wings of the wind.

The mighty voice continued to speak drawing her ever nearer as it did. "Ameara, I call thee unto life, and unto all I have for thee. I have removed the old and have done a new work in thee. From this day forward, thou shall no longer be called Amanda, but Ameara. It is the name of a princess, for you are a child of your Father the King. I have called thee by thy name. Thou art mine."

In a moment of baffled perplexity, her head spinning, Amanda realized she was breathing. The water was swirling past her face and sides, yet there was also air; cool, clean air, far purer than that which had greeted her outside her sickroom. Its touch was the touch of life, and its sweetness brought healing to her damaged lungs. This could only be the work of the Father. He was fulfilling His promise as only He could.

In another second she had surfaced. The waves washed over her, but she rose again. It was as if a hand had hold of her shoulders and was pulling her up. The sky above was dark and blurred by clouds; but the air, it was not that of where she had been, or the place from whence she had been abducted. This was a different place, one of living things, yet not of illusion. She could see the trees from where she floated, rising and falling with the slope of the land, their green and flourishing crowns shaking in the wind. Their trunks were immense, some must have been nigh a hundred years old. They stood as if to welcome her to this new word, linked by their many arms and whispering in a language all their own. The smells of pine, cedar, aspen, oak, maple, and mulberry all mingled in a mixture of lively cheer. It felt like more than a dream. This place felt like home. A home to which she had never been, yet for which she had always longed.

    Though completely drained of strength, somehow, Amanda made it to the shore. Collapsing, she uttered out a single word. Thank you.

Chapter Twenty-six:
The Chase

The fleeing vehicle sped across the cracked and colorless ground. Behind it, past the trailing cloud of alkaline dust, the air-ships were closing in. The hills were still far off. There was no way they could outrun the enemy, yet they could not stop. The surrounding land was flat, hard, and barren, with no hope of shelter or concealment.

As Gillean keeps them flying at full throttle, Mathias takes hold of the tarp lying in the back of the rig. He yanks it away to reveal a weapon both intriguing and slightly frightening; A twenty-millimeter cannon. It is old, but the barrel looks to be made of solid brass. It is mounted on some sort of swiveling tripod. There is writing on the side of the barrel, words in a strange language which he cannot read. Mathias has seen writing of this kind before, yet he cannot remember where.

As the vehicle bounces and wind whips past his head, Mathias sees the approaching doom. Over the rush and roar of engines, he hears the scream of an owl man, and knows that he will have to use this archaic weapon. He unstraps his safety-belt. The vehicle hits a bump and the shock of it nearly sends him flying. He grips the rails for dear life reaching for the swiveling gun. Beneath it is a wooden crate marked "ordinance".

Mathias has literally no idea what he is doing. He had no training with weapons such as this, no background with the resistance. He has used a rifle before, yet, until very recently, his life has been one of pacifism, not violence. As he takes out one of the gleaming shells and holds it up, he briefly ponders how much damage it will do. How much life will this messenger remove? He has to keep reminding himself that they are fighting godless, demonic monsters, and not mere men. He is glad they are not men like him, otherwise he might not be able to do what is needed.

Becoming aware of the weapon's existence, Gillean yells at him to hurry. This adds to the nervousness already biting at him, but he cannot let it stay his efforts. He almost drops the shell he is holding, but somehow manages to keep hold of it as they veer northward. He fumbles with what he believes is the bolt which will open the chamber. His world is sweat, and noise, and fear, and the stubborn bolt which will not budge. Working feverishly to loosen the worn metal, he calls out to the Father.

The thrum and roar of the air-ships is almost on top of them now. They have not yet opened up on them with thier guns. Gillean believes this is because they wish to take them alive. He has no intention of permitting this.

Gillean turns in his seat, still keeping his foot pressed tight against the gas. He raises the revolver of his dead wife with defiance in his eyes. A wild, blood-curdling cry escapes his lips and he pulls the trigger.

The shots ring out in rapid succession, most of them striking their intended target. He knows where to aim, at the corner of the windshield where the glass is thinnest. The Assembly builds strong and formidable air-ships, yet they cut corners and Gillean knows this.

The large locust-shaped craft slows, then descends, skimming the dusty ground before tipping nose first, and exploding in a bloom of bright flames.

Gillean turns back to face the darkening plain before them. Still keeping one hand glued to the wheel, he tries to quickly reload with the other. There is the sound of metallic thunder, and a tracer-bolt flares past them. Others come racing down, pulverizing the bone-hard salt flats of the dead land.

Now he is swerving, careening to the right and then the left, watching the rearview mirror and praying his friend will learn to use the cannon before they are turned to scrap metal and raw meat.

As if on cue, there is a clank from the back seat. Mathias has successfully chambered a round and is attempting to aim the massive gun. Gillean knows he must be shaking like a leaf as he reaches for the lever. He prays for Mathias's hands and the steadying of his nerves. He does not know how many shells they have, but he doubts they will have time to use many. The tracers are punching closer and closer to their tires, closing in from both sides in a pulsing arch of blinding death.

There is a belch of sound and the vehicle leapt into the air. The jarring force of their landing was enough to rattle their bones. For a second, Gillean feared their tires would blow, but they remained intact.

Behind them, the dimming sky was alight with fire and falling debris. The shell had struck the craft to their left dead center. It had instantly spiraled out of control, swinging into the one on the right. They had exploded together, two metal birds made one in a flare of flames.

Gillean shouted and raised his fist in salute to his comrade. He praised Mathias for the shot, and laughed like one who has just been given back his life. Mathias, however, could not hear him. The noise of the blast had temporarily taken away the use of his ears. He remained crouched against the backseat, but was able to raise his head enough to mouth the words, "I'm all right."

The other ground vehicles had pulled back. They looked as if they might even break off the pursuit. It was getting truly dark now, and the peaks which had seemed distant were beginning to rise tall and towering up ahead. Just a little way yet to go, and they would find shelter for the night. Maybe, if the fuel held out, they might even make it most of the way back home. So relieved and excited were they over their victory that they did not see the shadowed form walking out into their path.

The old woman wore a black, hooded mantle. Her wrinkled face was ancient, almost noble in the way she held her gaze. Yet behind those dark, spectacled eyes, there was no virtue; no kindness or righteous-minded wisdom. She did not share such "weaknesses". Her desires were death, and the control and confinement of all sentient life.

Lillith hated all life, but most particularly men. She blamed them for the destruction of her world; their haughtiness, their injustice, their cruel treatment of women. Yet she had become far crueler still; oh yes, she had become a terror. Not a man living knew the true meaning of distress, till he gazed into her burning, hate-filled eyes and had felt her cold, boney fingers round his throat.

At one time, she had been no more than a wraith, an outcast among Hector's servants. Yet now, she had come into her own, for she had partnered with the devourer.

That great, silent yet ravenous wolf had found her sitting amongst the potshards, picking at her many sores. He had lowered his black and bristling head, showing her his jaws, and she had known why had had chosen her. He wished for her to feed him, and feed him she would. She had vowed to be his herald and helper. She would be the one to go before, preparing his way, and opening the doors for him that he might devour freely all who cowered within. She had become the handmaiden of death.

Now, as she faced this loud and reckless thing barreling across her wasteland, she was not daunted. She knew these fools. She could see God's light on them as clearly as she could see the shadow of evil rising over this world. The one was golden, but the other, oh yes, he had venom in his veins. There was a hatred in him whether he realized it or not, and she would make the most of it. It had been far too long since she had strangled a man. This would be a night she would long remember, and revel in the recollections thereof.

The vehicle had slowed, yet they were still going a goodly speed above what was safe. The first thing Gillean saw of the old witch was her face. Two beetle-black eyes peered out at him from a face of grizzled flesh.

Instantly, he recognized her from his nightmares. He slammed on the brakes, yet they were already too near her for escape.

Lillith raised her arms, fists clenched, nails digging into her palms. The front of the vehicle rose into the air. They were flipped backwards, like a child's toy. Mathias was thrown clear, but Gillean remained inside the tumbling wreck. It came crashing down in a broken heap upon the calloused earth. Miraculously, the fuel tanks did not explode.

In the stillness following the crash, the night gathered in around. Somewhere, far up in the hills, an owl hooted. Nothing moved, nothing save for the wind and an old, hooded woman, meandering through the darkness.

Chapter Twenty-seven:
The Light

It took a few minutes for Gillean's mind to catch up with his body. Everything had happened so fast. His heart hammered against the wall of his chest, and there was a stabbing pain in his left flank. He could not see clearly, but that was not surprising. He believed this was more due to the darkness than anything else. It was very dark. The sky had passed from dimly glowing canvas, to a clouded void without moon or stars.

At first, Gillean as afraid to move, dreading what injuries he might discover. He was suspended, hanging upside down from his safety belt. The blood was rushing to his head and he was beginning to feel faint, yet he knew he could not remain this way. He had to find Mathias.

He could feel both his legs now, and neither of them were broken. He might have busted some ribs, yet that remained to be seen. He called out for Mathias, but there was no response, only the wind whistling against the crumpled metal.

Carefully, Gillean drew out the smaller of his two knives and proceeded to cut himself loose. He tried not to think of what might have befallen his friend; yet, the thoughts pushed through on their own. Images of Mathias's thin, care-worn face flooded his mind. He saw him lying in a pool of blood, both legs broken, his neck snapped, and twisted at an unnatural angle. These gruesome visions haunted him, compelling him to waste no time. Even if the other man was dead, he had to know. If he was seriously injured, time might prove crucial.

It was then, Gillean realized, he had grown tired of being alone. In many ways, he had become accustomed to isolation; yet in this man, he had found a friend, and he was beginning to understand what that was worth.

Grabbing hold of one of the rails, Gillean succeeded in freeing himself. He swung down like a spider monkey, nearly catching his right foot on the steering wheel as he did. He was thankful that he had tucked his revolver back into his belt before the crash. There was no sign of his pack. It must have flown out when they flipped.

He called out for Mathias again, then stopped short. Suddenly, the image of a ghostly, hooded face was reborn in his mind. The old woman, Lillith, this was her doing! She had intended to be the death of them.

Gillean's respirations increased, and his eyes darted to and fro in the darkness. Slowly, his fingers twitching, he reached for the revolver. He had encountered this woman before. She was not one to leave her work unfinished. With solemn dread, he recalled the words of one once cursed by her.

"She never leaves a task unfinished for long. She may not always be swift, but her devices are never weak in their working. When she predicts your death, she is never wrong."

The man had died with these words upon his lips. He had fled this life with fear in his eyes and the witch's curse burning upon his brow.

"Greater is He who is in me than, he who is in the world," Gillean whispered as he searched.

The pain in his side was still there, yet it did not concern him. He could not find Mathias anywhere. He turned back towards the wreck, and that was when she came for him.

The old witch lunged out of the darkness. For the briefest moment, Gillean thought he could see the snout and livid eyes of a monstrous wolf. Then she was upon him, seizing his hands and driving him back with the force of a howling hurricane.

The revolver was wrenched from his hand, and he was cast to the ground like a piece of rubbish. Before he could draw out his knife, his arms were pinned and her hands were around his neck. They were stronger than steel and felt like burning ice. The nails dug into his skin, sending rivulets of dark blood trickling down onto his shirt. In her eyes, he could see the flames of the world beneath. They raged, yet were never sated. They consumed, yet were never quenched.

As he lay dying in the witch's grasp, a vision coursed through his mind. He saw the eyes of his darling beloved, her beautiful face consumed with pain. Once again, he was forced to witness her death, slower, more agonizing than he had remembered it, yet to him, none the less real. He cried for her, every fiber of his being wishing to hold her in his arms and comfort her. Yet now he could not. This time he was distant, aloof, unable to give her anything but the unconscious prayers of his tortured soul.

At that moment, Gillean lost all will to fight. He wanted to die, believed that he deserved to. What had he given in this life but the failings of a wayward man: a man who has once desired to be righteous, but has allowed the world in which he resides to corrupt him and fill him with bitterness and remorse. He is a man who has lost all those for which he once cared; a man who has outlived his purpose.

As if sensing his grief, Lillith leans in close, her dust-smeared spectacles glowing with the eerie illumination of her horrid soul. Her lips begin to move. Gillean does not hear the words, yet he knows them all the same.

"How tragic, this shameful sight, a man who has outlived his purpose; a half of a broken whole, left destitute amongst the wreckage. You have lost your witness. You will never see those you love again. In this knowledge, disperse and flee this mortal coil."

She presses harder. They are no longer alone. Beside the wretched witch stands a great and burly beast. His narrow eyes flare red against the black. His mouth opens to reveal row upon row of razor-sharp teeth, obsidian and crimson with the blood of thieves and saints alike. He is the devourer, the one who consumes. He is waiting to be fed.

What happened next was neither expected nor fully understood. There was a brilliant flash which seemed to come from all around them. The old woman let go of Gillean's throat and stumbled back. With a shuddering howl, the wolf vanished, unable to tolerate the searing light.

From behind him, Gillean heard a voice speak loud and strong. It was Mathias. Sudenly, he realized, the light was with him. It was not flowing from him, but through him, as if he were a portal.

"The eternal God is thy refuge, and underneath are the everlasting arms. He shall thrust out the enemy before thee; and shall say destroy them."

The old witch fled into the night, shrieking like a banshee. She knew there she was outmatched. This was the work of the Father.

Chapter Twenty-eight:
Alman Freemont

Alman Freemont was working in his southern field. He seemed tireless in his labors. The truth was that he enjoyed them. Though a veteran of many years, he still moved like a younger man, hefting his long-handled hoe, stripping away the weeds from the soil.

Though he lacked the stature common to his people, he had the respect of them all. Most of them were farmers, yet Alman was something more. He was one of the Kem, a line of holy men, stewards of the land known as the center reach.

Like his father before him, he was esteemed as a leader. All the communities and villages looked to him for guidance, for he walked closely with God. He was a man of his word, honest and noble. Time and again he had proven himself through his council and skills as a peacemaker. Most who knew him were somehow indebted to his wisdom. They had wanted to make him their king. Alman had often laughed inwardly at this. It had been so long since these people had known real rulers. He was sure they had no idea what this would mean. If they had, they might have very well kept their mouths shut. In any case, he was always swift to remind them from whence his virtues flowed.

Alman took his duties as a Kem priest seriously, every bit as seriously as the tending of his crops. He enjoyed time spent working and walking amongst the fields, yet not on the sabbath. This day belonged to the Father. It was sacred and set aside, a time for contemplation and the study of the Word.

Though some considered them unnecessary, Alman still clung to the old ways. "Seek ye the old paths," his father used to say. "Seek ye out the old paths and so ye shall walk alright." This was what Alman truly believed. Their standards and traditions had been given them from God for a reason.

He feared the winds of change. He dreaded them, mostly because of the turmoil and possible destruction they would bring; yet they were coming all the same. There was a darkness rising in the east. Rumors of unrest and evil were spreading through the center reach, and already, many had begun to flee west.

For some, this seemed the best alternative, yet Alman knew this was not the will of the Father. This was their land; it had been since before time immemorial and they had been charged with its keeping and care.

Yes, they would be sent a ruler, a one chosen to shepherd them in time of trial. It had been prophesied that their long-awaited protector would come to them by a secret way. He man would come to them in the garb of a warrior, with the coat of a king. He would arrive at the house of the Elder Hall and would take possession of it. It was said that when smoke rose from the ancient center chimney, the time of his reign would be begun.

For the time being, the mighty house of Elder Hall stood empty. It stood on the land adjacent to Alman's farm, tall and majestic as ever, though overgrown by weeds and vines. It had remained vacant for nearly two hundred years, since the last protector of the realm had died, leaving no heir to carry on in his stead.

Alman's father, Ambrose Freemont, had cared for the great house, passing on the duty to his son. The farmer priest made sure the interior was well kept, swept and clean in anticipation of his master's arrival. The only thing he did not tend to was the growth surrounding the house. This was not his place. According to what had once been spoken, this would be attended to by the protector himself. Though it had been long, and doubt abounded in the minds of many, Alman believed the time of the prophecy's fulfillment was near at hand.

The Father knows our need. He thought as he continued to strike at the weeds. *He shall not leave us defenseless in the face of what is to come.*

Abruptly, his movements stopped. From beyond the rising stalks of spring-green corn there was the sound of horse's hooves. Gazing down the row in which he stood, Alman caught sight of his youngest daughter, Gaviene.

At first, he was concerned. It was usually one of the older children who was sent to fetch him when he was needed at the house. Yet, when he took note of her face, he knew all was well. It bore a look of exuberant excitement. Her smile glowed and her wide eyes sparkled in the sunlight.

"Father! Father! She's awake! The woman at home, she's awake!"

Chapter Twenty-nine: Conversing

The teak wood stairs creaked and groaned under the weight of Alman's feet. In one hand, he held a black, leather-bound book: in the other, a folded scrap of paper. Many questions buzzed within his mind, yet he was resolved to ask them carefully. He knew not whom they were dealing with after all. He thought he did, yet that remained to be seen.

Upon reaching the top of the stairs, he entered a long, dark hallway. Walking seven paces, he came to the first door on the right. Alman tucked the scrap of paper into the book and knocked. From inside, a voice bid him enter and he did.

The room was small, yet comfortable. It smelled of chamomile and sweet lamp oil. The light from the window caused the sky-blue walls to glow softly, and the white curtains flowed in the gentle breeze. This was a sacred room. It had seen its share of death, yet also life.

Two women were seated beside the bed. The first was Alman's second eldest daughter, Gaila. The other was their guest, the young woman who called herself Ameara.

They had found her on the shore of the gray sea. She had taken in quite a bit of water, had almost drowned from the look of her. Alman had feared she would die, and yet, somehow, he had known she wouldn't. He had carried her back to his house; and for nearly a week, his wife and daughters had tended to her, feeding her tea, water, and broth from a spoon. This was the first time she had been strong enough to sit up.

Alman bid the women good morning, removing his hat as he did. Moving slowly, he pulled up a third chair and sat down, letting his hat fall to the floor beside him. He noticed Ameara's blue eyes and how they widened when she saw the black book. Instinctively, she reached out for it; and he gave it to her, along with the worn scrap of paper. She took it with the greatest care, holding it up to inspect it in the light.

"It has taken long for it to dry, but dry it has. None of the pages have been damaged or ruined. I knew you would be wanting it."

"Thank, you good sir." Ameara said, giving a weak smile. "It is precious to me."

"The Word of the Father is precious. It is a joy and strength, a comfort in time of sorrow and a light to those who walk through darkness. Tell me, is it available in abundance where you hail from? We have not many copies here. It has been many years since we had a working press and most of our scribes have passed on. Is it revered in your country, cherished as it is here?" The older man seemed almost like a child in his excited queries.

"Those who seek it can still find it, most times at least, if God wills it. I'm sorry to say it is not widely available or widely reverenced. It was at one time, but no longer. My world has turned away from the Father."

Upon hearing this, Alman's face took on a look of grave sorrow. She could tell that he believed her, yet, there was still some confusion behind his eyes. She was surprised there was not more, considering the circumstances.

"How did the falling away occur?" He asked. "When did thy people turn their backs on God?"

"To tell the truth, I'm really not sure. There was so much confusion in what people believed. It was as if they could not decide what was real and what was not. The church tried to educate them, yet everyone knew they were hypocrites and put no faith in what they preached. I think there had been a distance growing for some time, between God and the people, that is. It was a slow turning, a gradual falling away. One of those things that no one noticed until it was done."

"So, their hearts turned cold?"

"Yes. I guess you could say that." But there was no guess about it. She had seen the destruction of her former world in her dreams. She had seen children ripped from the arms of their parents, and parents forsake their children. She had witnessed a time of lovelessness and fear, and she knew: this was the portion of those who forget their God.

"We began to care about other things," she said, "things that should not have mattered, but somehow did because we caused them to. We threw away what was precious and esteemed what was foolish. We made mockeries of the truth and followed after perversions. We, we made other gods to worship."

"You say...we?" Alman's face was still one of sadness, yet now, there was a cold steel forming behind his eyes. If she didn't know better, Ameara might have guessed that it was the beginnings of hate.

"I was, at one time, one of them. I thought I was doing the will of the Father, yet I deceived myself; but no more. He has given me grace, and I am not who I was. I failed Him and almost died because of it, yet He preserved me. I had to be broken and lose everything in order to fully understand the depths of his love."

"Father, please, do not ask much more of her concerning this." Gaila's voice seemed on the verge of tears. "She has spoken much in her dreams and more she has told to me. It is enough to know she has suffered and her faith has been restored."

"That it is," Alman agreed. The steel had fled his eyes and they were gentle once again.

"It's all right," Ameara said, almost apologetically. "You've taken me in and cared for me as if I was one of your own. The least I can do is to tell you how I came to be here."

Alman looked at her gravely, yet there was a twinkle in his eye. "My child, I already know how you came to our world. It is no secret to me, for I am of the Kem, a priest of the Most High. He walks with me and talks with me along the narrow way. He has told me of all your trials."

Amanda looked taken aback, almost fearful, yet Alman continued, unabated. "I must be honest with you, your arrival was not unexpected. You are indeed the first, yet, you shall not be the last. The Father shall send whom He wills, and those whom He sends, He sends with a purpose." He spoke with surety, as if it had already happened, this great arrival of persons unknown.

"What purpose?"

"Ah, this is to be seen." The solemnity of Alman's face had been replaced with something akin to amusement. "Yet, I can say this, His Word shall not return unto Him void. I feel that thou was meant to teach. The Word followed you here. The Father has placed a great calling upon your shoulders. He sees and knows your love for Him, and for others. Your devotion to Him is without question. It is he who has called thee by thy name. He has given thee a new one, is that not so?"

Ameara, formerly Amanda, nodded and Alman smiled.

"We are in need of those who will help us teach the Word. I do what I can, yet I am only one and there are many needing guidance. We could greatly use thy help."

"I, I would be honored, yet, I always thought, that is, I was always told it was a man's place to teach the scriptures."

"You did not let that hinder you when you ministered to your fellow captives."

"There was no one else to do so. I did as I was led to do."

"And so, you must do now. My child, call not unclean what God hath made clean. Let none stand in the way of your purpose. The Father is greater than man. If He says you may teach, then teach you shall. Surely, he shall send men to aid in the work, yet it was you He sent first. I believe there is a reason for this."

As they spoke, Ameara had continued to leaf through the pages of the Word. At that moment, a small, withered flower fell from between the pages. It alighted on her dress, then rolled off onto the floor. Before she had time to fully realize what it was, Gaila retrieved it. She held it for a moment, then offered it back to her with a knowing smile. It was feverfew, the one plant Ameara thought she might never see again.

"A gift from your beau," she said. "We boiled most of it to make a tea for you. It brought down your fever."

Alman's eyes twinkled more brilliantly than before. "Ah, yes. Feverfew. It is rare here abouts, truly it is. We have other herbs that serve the same purpose, but not quite as well, not by my reckoning at least. Your friend Gillean, it was he who sent you it, did he not?"

"I, I don't know. I suppose so."

"It says so in the letter," Gaila said, pointing to the folded scrap of paper Ameara had placed upon the bed.

"I do apologize. It should not have been read. My younger sisters were curious. They thought it might give us some clue as to who you were. This fellow Gillean, he seems very concerned for you. Will he be coming here as well?"

"I don't know." Ameara's face seemed puzzled, yet inside, she was aquiver with excitement. He had not forgotten her. He had sent her the feverfew to help her after all. Surely, his prayers to the Father had played a role in her deliverance from Hector.

"Mayhaps he shall." said Alman, gazing past the glowing walls to realms far beyond their reach. "Mayhaps he shall."

Chapter Thirty:
The Servant

Gillean had never considered himself a skeptic, one who questioned with or without evident cause. Yet, when Lillith's fingers wrapped around his throat, he had found himself questioning a great many things.

They say that death, real impending death, has a way of transforming one's mind. Some men are made stronger in its shadow, others weaker. There had been many a time when Gillean would not have resisted, but welcomed it. However, in the rancid grasp of those wicked claws, his desire to live had never been more ardent. All at once, death had seemed so cold, so unforgiving and final: a blind sleep in a shallow, forgotten grave.

He knew his soul had been secured, written firmly within the Father's book of life. Yet, what if there was more to salvation than this? What if something had been overlooked? The terrible uncertainty had been every bit as frightening as the witch herself. In retrospect, it could have simply been another part of her assault, an attack against the mind as well as the body. Yet, it troubled him all the same.

A part of him felt as if he had spent much too much time allowing himself to be troubled by thoughts and occurrences; but what could you expect in a world spiraling downward to oblivion? Reason and virtue had been routed and death was king. They were headed for a final cataclysm, one which would finish man's untimely work and erase this world for good. From what Gillean could tell, it was inevitable, a prophecy long since set in time-worn stone. If the world and all in it could be saved from destruction, what then was their purpose?

Without another thought, the still, small voice came flooding in to answer him. "To glorify the Father," it said, not chidingly, yet with a fair amount of emphasis. "To honor and praise Him, no matter what the circumstance. This is the purpose of life."

Gillean picked himself up, vowing in his heart of hearts that he would not forget this wisdom. He had known it once, yet like so much else, it had slipped away from him. Self-centeredness had played a role. Its self-imposed lie had been his undoing before. In light of the grace he had received, it behooved him to cast it off. He could ill afford to give into it again.

After Mathias had rescued him, he had told Gillean of a vision he had received from the Father. Gillean was forced to admit that, under other circumstances, he would have questioned this. The fellow had just been flung from a vehicle after all. He might have hit his head. Yet, seeing the light, he had known better. The light was of the Father, and could not be blasphemed without dire consequence. He had seen men struck dead for much less.

As soon has he had seen that marvelous light, he had known; this man was no mere preacher, he was a prophet of the Most High. Why he had been chosen to walk with such a one was beyond him. Surely, there were braver souls, stronger, far more devout than he. Yet this was what the Father had decided, and this was what would be.

Mathias had told him that they had been given a task. They were to travel into the heart of what had once been Assembly lands. They were to travel on until they reached the pass of Akron and its haunted narrow gates. This was the entry point to the forbidden city, the legendary capital of the Sacred Assembly itself: Arius. At those sad and evil gates, they would encounter a true terror; the false god of which the tamandua had spoken. What they would do upon viewing him, Mathias knew not. Yet, of one thing he was sure. There were those held under its sway who were in need of deliverance.

"This journey will in no way be easy," Mathias had said. The boldness and authority in his voice had surprised Gillean. "There is no guarantee we will survive when it is done. What we are promised is, if we would serve the Father, we must make haste. Our time is short and the evil is growing even as we speak."

Gillean had agreed to follow him. What else could he have done? He owed this man his life. He had spared him great hurt, not once, not twice, but thrice. It had been he who had broken the creature's spell at the old church in Gaven post. I had been he who had led him through the gnashing mob, and he who had delivered him from the clutches of the witch, with the power of God, of course. If there had been any doubt in Gillean's mind, it had long since flown. Mathias was a prophet and a saint and Gillean was called to be his servant.

The thought that the younger man was now his master troubled him not at all. In fact, he felt honored. Ever since Gillean had lost his wife, he had harbored a secret fear; a fear that the Father might be finished with him, that there was no plan or purpose left for him in this dark world. Now, he realized how foolish that thought had been, how ridiculous and immature. Everything which drew breath had a purpose. It was the completion of that inspired design which mattered. Surely, it was so for him; and Gillean was bound and determined to fulfill his purpose, no matter what the final cost.

Now, as they headed east, God's voice had never been so clear. All those who would have called them crazy for the heeding of His words were dead, or far removed. The fears and conflictions had been removed, and in their stead was given soundness of mind and stalwart resolve. They were told to be humble, yet granted boldness. They were encouraged in their steps, yet cautioned against pitfalls. Surely, there would be temptations and evils ahead of them, yet they would trust in the name of the Most High. To the Father, they would sing their truest praise.

Chapter Thirty-one:
Dregs

The sky had darkened since first light. Rolling clouds of angry gray pressed in from the horizon, like waves across a winter sea. Before, the wind had followed them; now it confronted them in raging gusts.

There were trees here, but not many, and none of them living. The remnants of the old forests were shattered and bleached. They stood at odd angles, like toothpicks or derelict fence posts left to rot. A few small birds still flitted through their dusty limbs, taking refuge in holes and hollows. Yet, aside from these there was no life. The poisons of men and war had done their work fell.

Amongst these dead and ruined woodlands, they came across a road, and near it, the remains of what had once been a small town. Klideburn was its name. Gillean thought he remembered it from his younger years. Like most living, growing things in this world, its population had disappeared. Its people had either perished or fled north to join the settlements of that land.

They had passed several small groups headed that way. They had consisted of mostly women, along with some older men. They had said that everyone was headed north and that it was the only logical place to go. There was rumored to be something there, a place of refuge they referred to as the Cave. Gillean had never before heard of "the Cave," yet, its very mention sent cold shivers down his spine. The name felt dark, and overwhelmingly unpleasant. Every sense inside him told him it was not a place of safety, but rather confinement. He hoped these travelers knew what they were doing. Somehow, he did not believe they did.

"You'll see them again," said a haunting and familiar voice from deep inside his head. "In their darkest hour, you shall see them. Mayhap it will be your darkest hour as well, and the epitaph of your shame. Does it not hollow out your heart, knowing that your greatest pain is yet to come?"

*My heart has already been hollowed out, h*e thought, *and filled with life more abundant than you will ever know.*

"But of course, I forgot, you no longer have a heart. This world ate it up, destroyed it after I took from you your reason for living. Tell me, how did she look when she died, when her pale face turned cold one last time? She shall remain cold forever. It was how she was and how she will always be. It's how you shall remember her."

"Be silent!" Gillean roared inside his mind. "In the name of the Father, of precious Jesus, and of His Spirit, you shall speak to me no more!"

His leg was starting to throb again. The weighty pack he carried was beginning to weigh him down. Suddenly, all things seemed worthless and futile. This world was dying, nearly dead. What were they doing here?

"Is all well, Gillean?" Mathias had turned and was studying his face. This was a habit of his. Whenever he sensed there was something amiss, he would hone in on one's features, as if trying to read between the lines. When they first met, this had annoyed Gillean to no end, yet now, he did not mind. There was genuine concern in his young master's question, and although it was a question, it was as if Mathias had already guessed his thoughts.

"Just fighting my demons. Trying to keep them at bey. Had to invoke the Spirit of God."

"Just because they trouble you, doesn't mean you have to claim them." Mathias smiled knowingly. "Be at peace. You aren't deranged. I could hear him as well. The deceiver would set his face against both of us."

"You mean Hector?" Gillean was surprised to hear himself speak the name. It had been long since he had.

"Aye, the very same. The man of shadows. Master of shadows some call him." Mathias glanced around as if expecting their adversary to suddenly appear. "Most call him Hector, and well named he is, for he would harry the people of God and would hector us until we turn aside from our way. He would bind us with fear and encompass us with sorrows, using our past failing against us. Yet, always remember, every word he speaks is rooted in a lie. Give no place to him Gillean, for the thief is come only to kill, steal, and destroy."

"How well I know," Gillean replied, looking down as he did. "Through my negligence, I've suffered much at his hand. He's taken more from me than I ever thought he would: more than I ever thought the Father would allow. Yet, God willing, I may one day have my revenge."

"What the devil has taken, the Father shall restore. This He would bid me speak to you. It is his solemn promise, given unto thee. No matter how dark the night, you shall see His words fulfilled before your death."

"Thank you for this, and thanks be to the Father," said Gillean, still looking down.

"Why do you doubt? You know I speak truth."

"I do not doubt you, or the faithfulness of the Father. It's just hard for me to understand. I had love, and I had a life, a wife, a home, a purpose. It was all ripped away. I've fallen so far. I, I know He still cares for me and for my soul; I simply don't see how things could ever be good again, not in this world."

Gillean looks around at the dead and wind tossed trees, the broken road lined with glass and debris. It has been so long since love, real love has lived fully in his heart. Not just the love a man has for woman, but the care and compassion which the true believer feels for those he sees around him; the love that once sustained his world.

"Though you doubt and struggle to believe, the word spoken by the Father shall not change. His covenant with you will He not break, nor will He alter the thing which has gone out of His mouth. Concerning vengeance, that belongs to him. The Father has prepared an end for Hector. He shall not escape his judgment day."

"Tell me true," said Gillean, his eyes alive with living flame, "if the Father stands with me, will I be able to vanquish Hector. Will I be able to best the Devil?"

Mathias stared at him long and hard with his most piercing gaze. It was difficult to know what he was thinking. For a moment, Gillean wondered if he had spoken wrong. Had not his master just finished advising him not to make revenge his focus? Yet Gillean's need to face the shadowed man was more than mere desire. It was necessity. He understood, had known for years that Hector wished to place a claim upon his life. The only way he would ever find rest, perhaps restore his innermost self, was to vanquish this dark and sinister man. Surely, his master must understand this.

"Only the Father can say." was his reply. "If He be for thee, there is none who can stand against thee."

"And if I fail Him as before?"

Gillean felt he already knew the answer, yet he wanted to hear his friend speak it all the same.

"If we depart, He abideth faithful," Mathias spoke mater of factly, "but you will never have the victory."

They had stopped beside the rugged road, and Gillean had been able to remove the heavy pack from off his shoulders. The chance to rest was a blessing, one they both sorely needed.

Ahead of them, the abandoned town waited beneath the promise of a storm. It seemed to crouch like a black cat on a moonless night, as if waiting to pounce upon unsuspecting travelers. They could feel the decaying presence cutting at their souls, sick and rotting, and filthy like a living death. Here was yet another rancid realm, one more of those anathemas which seemed to blight their path. Klideburn had itself become a curse, the dregs of a subverted earth.

The gloom and chill emanating from those haunted streets and houses was stalking them. It was at one point so intense that Gillean felt the urge to sing, if only to hold back the ghostly vibe. Yet he dared not raise his voice. Something told him that there were more than skeletons amongst those ruined homes. There was danger here.

"Aye, the Spirit speaks expressly concerning what lies ahead." Mathias's voice was barely audible above the moaning wind. "We must be on our guard. This is another Spiderback, a habitation of owls, a dwelling place for demons. It is in places such as these that the spirits of enmity choose to congregate. We must pass through quickly, taking nothing from this place, not even water."

Gillean agreed. He had almost suggested that they go around the town, avoiding it all together. Yet, this would take time; precious time which, according to Mathias, they did not have to spare. In addition to this, he was not sure evading its borders would keep them safe. The ghostly aura of the place seemed to swell. It spread out on either side of the road like a doleful, creeping mist; the type of mist in which one might become lost and perish in parts unknown.

Gillean shouldered his pack. He felt for the butt of his pistol, making sure it was still there. He had the gnawing feeling he would be forced to use it soon. As he prayed for courage, it came to him, yet carefulness still kept his steps in check. They were entering the dregs, the wreckage of what once knew hopeful life.

Almost as soon as they passed the first house, Gillean understood; he realized the origin of their dread. This place had been consumed. The devourer had made a bloody supper here.

Chapter Thirty-two:
The Devourer

As they made their way through the empty streets of Klideburn, the pressure of the place began to mount, just as Gillean had known it would. He could feel the huddled homes closing in on him. Their windows looked like the gaping eyes of skulls, unblinking in their vacant darkness. Doors hung and swung from rusty hinges, left open for the wind to play with. The clack they made as they struck set his teeth on edge.

The boldness granted them was waning. They struggled to keep it, yet it continued to fade with each and every step. The rising dread of the dregs was all around them now. It was as it had been in the hills, yet now, it was stronger. The aura seemed more certain this time, as if death was just a footfall away.

Gillean was determined to stay by his master, yet he wanted out of this town. Everything inside of him was screaming that they should not be here. The warnings were relentless and unyielding. Somewhere in the outskirts, they had crossed over a faded line and had entered into a realm which had been damned. Whether this damning came about by the sins of its people, or by those of others, Gillean could not say; yet the edict stood, and the very thought of it made his skin crawl. Only by sheer resolve did he fight back the urge to run. Caution was still needed. Nevertheless, they both quickened their steps and prayed that they would reach the other side 'ere long.

All throughout the yards and ruined streets, random objects had been strewn. They had been thrown down, broken, as if forsaken in great haste: a shattered dish, a battered book, a mangled string of children's toys. Farther along, a music box, its frame crushed, its gears scattered in the rusty dirt. These were the leavings of another life, another world before; things which made the heart grow sick. "What is once lost is lost forever," an old poet had once stated. Here in dregs, this was all too true. The foundations had been removed, and this was what remained, that hideous cancer which had grown beneath the skin.

If Hector had his way, the entirety of their world would become like this, void and vacant. But yet, this was not quite true. He would retain some life. The subjugation of living souls was just as much a part of his sadistic nature as destruction. What then would his altered world be, a prison, a realm of perpetual torment, perhaps even an extension of Hell itself?

Gillean shook his head, attempting to clear it of less than helpful thoughts. In truth, it did no good to dwell on such things, certainly not in a time like this. He needed something else, something beautiful to think upon. In his mind's eye, he recalled Amanda, the woman from his dreams. He thought of her lovely blue eyes, and her long, dark hair soft against the curve of her face and neck. Mayhaps, someday he would see her in person.

Suddenly, Gillean looked up to see that Mathias had stopped. He was standing up ahead of him and slightly to the left, beside an old wrought-iron gate. Gillean wished to remind him of his own words, that they should waste no time and pass through quickly. Yet, he did not. Instead Gillean realized something had caught the other man's attention.

Against the black and rusty gate lay a framed portrait. It was wide, and Gillean could tell that, at one time, it had been beautiful. Yet now its face was gone, torn away by the marks of massive, rending claws.

On its lower half, written in what might have been blood, was a queer and chilling rhyme. It read, "Fear the wolf, his fangs are red. He consumes all things which are not dead. Though you feed him, he is never full. He ever hungers for your soul."

Gillean was not sure he understood, and yet, in a way he did.

Life is in the blood, and blood is red. The creature is more than just a killer, it consumes life. There are many demons which eat away at life, but only one which devours everything. Devours! The devouring spirit! The spirit of the devourer! He consumes everything and his hunger is never sated; but what he craves most are human souls, and he waiting, he's waiting here for us!

Again, he turned his attention to Mathias, hoping that he would be ready to move. Yet, the man remained still, as still as stone. With an anger kindled by fear, Gillean reached out and grasped his master's shoulder. Only, it was not Mathias standing beside him, it was a statue; a hooded, solitary statue which had endured there since before the town was born.

Somehow, Gillean had lost sight of his master, and had been left behind. He opened his mouth, but he had no words, only a numbness in his bones, and a paranoid sensation that something unseen was creeping up on him. It was then that he saw the bodies.

They lay in the street, side by side, shoulder to shoulder. They were of all age: men, women, and children. With a pang of bitter shock, Gillean realized that they had all been slain recently. Not so long ago, there had been people still living here.

The head and hands of each corpse had been removed. In lieu of the pale-gray pallor of death, their skins were chalk white. Something had drained them of their blood.

In that horrific instant, all the stories, all the fabled wives-tales of his youth came flooding back to Gillean. The air had become stiflingly hot. There appeared to be a dull and dreadful red light arising from somewhere just out of sight. There was a moment, after the wind died, when even his own beating heart seemed to have stopped.

Gathering what courage he had left, Gillean stepped forward. He squared his shoulders and drew in a lung full of hot air, also drawing his gun. He looked for a path among the dead, yet found none. He would have to wade through them, there was no other way forward. Keeping as far as he could from the darkened doorways, he began to make his way through the morbid swamp of lifeless forms. It was not easy, yet somehow, he managed. All the while, he listened for the monster.

About half-way through the sea of decapitated bodies, he heard an unsettling sound. It was harsh and abrasive to the senses. It sounded like the grinding of teeth. Gillean found himself directly in front of an old store. Its rusted metal awning leaned to one side, and its wide front window had been shattered. Above the awning was a large, hand-painted sign which read "mercantile." Suddenly, he remembered it. He had been here before, had once been inside this very store. The feeling was bone-chilling to say the least.

All at once, he was caught up in the anomaly. The vision of what had been washed over him in flares of puckered flame. He saw the towns people as they had been, their faces flushed, their eyes wide with naked terror. In the soiled light, Gillean watched what had at one time befallen them.

Through the wide window, now unbroken, he saw men and women scurrying back and forth. They were grabbing everything they could carry. They ransacked the shelves and counters, smashing glass cases and sending cans of food clattering across the floor.

From the center of town, a bell clanged wildly. The looters looked up, their terrified expressions frozen in place. Like animals, they resumed their pillaging, more violently than before. No one helped his or her neighbor. In the shadow of destruction, it was everyone for themselves.

Frightened cries came wailing from all around. Men were running past him now, screaming like little children, forgetting their families. An enormous black shape was pursuing them. The creature moved so quickly, Gillean could not distinguish much concerning its features. It was covered in thick fur which appeared to shed and follow it as a cloud. Its back and shoulders were arched in a grotesque hump; and it looked like a bear, but for its long and limber legs.

In a split-second maneuver, the thing broke off its pursuit and barreled towards the mercantile. The door, which had been shut, was flung wide as if someone had pushed it open to welcome the monster. Later, when he had more time to think, Gillean realized he had seen a pale hand doing that very thing. Yet, there was no time for reflection now. The monster was inside, tearing apart the place in a way the desperate looters could never have accomplished.

Bodies flew through the air, along with victuals and garments rolled in blood. Though he stood outside with the pulsing flames, Gillean saw each and every event simultaneously almost as if he was experiencing it himself. It was a nightmare.

A man had fallen in the chaos. He was older, probably in his mid to late sixties. From the look of his clothes, he appeared to have been fairly well-to-do. His fine suit was now soiled with blood as he wriggled backwards across the slippery floor. In one hand, he clutched a revolver; in the other a silk money purse.

The dark beast turned its attention towards him, its eyes flashing a decaying shade of burning yellow. It bared its reddened teeth and Gillean realized what it was. It was a wolf, a gargantuan canine as big as a horse. Its ears were pinned back and its head swayed from side to side as it approached its prey.

The doomed man let out a hollow, gurgling shriek. Raising his gun, he fired shot after shot, but to no avail. Trembling on the verge of tears, he began to plead with the monster, as if it could understand him.

"Please, don't eat me! You can have anything, everything you want! Take my wife! Take my daughter. They are more tender than I!"

In truth, Gillean was not totally surprised when the beast answered him.

"I have consumed them already. They were just as hollow as you."

"Please, no!" wailed the man. "I want to live! Here, take my money! You can have my money!"

The man opened his silk purse and began to throw fist fulls of coins and bills at the beast, before finaly tossing the entire purse in his direction. He looked like an idiot, a fool devoid of understanding. Gillean knew he would die as such.

Not waiting to witness the man's grisly fate, Gillean bolted over the remainder of the headless corpses. He could see the edge of town up ahead. It glowed with the failing light of dusk, just beyond the leaning walls. He had to move quickly. Somehow, he knew the anomaly was not a lie. It was an analogue, a recording, a story which had been set down as part of the enduring curse. If he tarried any longer, he would become part of it; and if he did not, the creature would claim his life all the same. He knew it was still here. He could feel its breath, the warm rasping prickle of its exhalations. It was still ravenous, and it would be so until the world died, or God saw fit to purge its evil being from existence.

    He felt the fire grab for him, and could have sworn the road was resisting his steps. It seemed to grow longer, putting more distance between him and that patch of sky which was his hope. Gillean prayed as he ran. The words came to him swiftly with the beating of his heart. He cried out for strength, for purity, for a sound mind. Most of all, he cried out for guidance. Survival was not what mattered in the end, it was the fulfilling of the Father's purpose. He had been called unto life for a reason; and, God willing, that reason would lead him unto life.

    He was almost there. Just a few more steps and then...Gillean's blood ran cold once again. The devourer had barred his path.

Chapter Thirty-three:
A Walk with the Sisters

The sky was gray again today, yet beautifully so. There was light between the clouds which let Ameara know the sun still lived. The shades and hues were real, alive with their own fullness. Even the dreariest aspects of this world held more brightness than those of her own. It was as if light and color mattered more here, as if they were woven into the nature of the place itself, as if they truly belonged. Ameara was beginning to feel as if she truly belonged here as well.

She had spent the day with Alman's daughters (Azalea, Gaila, Mosa, and Gaviene), her new friends. They had been quick to accept her as one of the family. This had surprised Ameara, who was accustomed to distrust. People from her home were neither this polite, nor this welcoming, especially to strangers. Yet, she knew they were genuine in their regard for her, and this blessed her soul. They were honest folk, yet uncommonly kind; and, for the most part, she felt completely at ease with them.

Most of the morning had been spent completing their designated chores. When these were done, they had all gone berry picking. Now, they walked the sandy slopes not far from where she had been found. From beyond a healthy line of oaks, they could hear the sound of the sea. The rise and fall of the rolling waves was restful. Gulls hovered on the wind, and from the wooded cliffs and hills to the north, songbirds trilled. It was the type of day you long to dream about.

Azalea, the eldest, had said that it might rain and that they should head back. Gaviene had informed her, not unkindly, that they were enjoying the weather and that it would take more than a little rain to frighten them away, so they continued on.

Out of all the Freemont sisters, Gaviene seemed to have taken a particular liking to their guest. On the long trek from the blueberry patch, she had wanted to hold her hand, remaining close to her as they worked. Ameara, who had always wanted a little sister, had been overjoyed. Odd though it seemed, she could not remember a time when the young girl had not been smiling. An angel child, some might have called her. Gaviene was always able to see the good in things. She was an encourager, a continual optimist. Her personality was unbridled by fear, or even the slightest bit of worry. Her sisters were convinced she could tame a tiger if she had to.

Mosa, the second youngest, spoke little; yet was always ready to lend help where she was needed. Though not as brave and bold as her other sisters, she was equally as kind. Mosa was the deep thinker, the ponderer of mysteries. Often, whilst her sisters were discussing a matter, she would keep silent, only waiting until they were done to speak her peace. Most times, there was great wisdom in her words.

Ameara wondered if such people had ever existed in her old world. At one time, they might have. She wondered how these young women would have turned out if they had been forced to live her life. She shuddered to think of how it might have changed them.

She answered their questions as best she could, their queries concerning her past life. Alman had asked her not to speak to them of the Assembly or of the evils which she had experienced. Gaila knew most of it already, and Gaviene had overheard some of her nightmares, yet, it was understood that they were to inquire about these things no further.

Being a prudent man, Alman understood that he could not keep them sheltered for long. Yet, while light still ruled in their land, he wished them not to fear. The days of terror would be upon them soon enough. Already, the shadow in the east was rising, beginning to spread. He had trained his sons in combat. He had not soiled their minds with the knowledge of the shadow, yet he had taught them to fight. They were away now, yet soon they would return to help him with the harvest. It had been hard on all of them since the passing of their mother

Adarrah, God rest her soul. He had told Ameara of her, how she had looked after them. He so wished she could have met her, had been here to greet her when she first arrived. Perhaps he sensed that Ameara had never known a true mother's love. He could sense a great many things, this was evident. It was also evident that he took great interest in the man with whom she had been corresponding. Alman seemed to believe that her fate and that of the man named Gillean, were somehow linked.

"Ameara," It was Gaila's voice calling her back from her reveries, "The books you mentioned before, the ones you used to read as a child; what were they about?"

"About common people mostly."

"None about magic. Castles and princes and far off kingdoms," Gaviene cut in.

"There were some like that, but most of them were stories about everyday people. People who found love, or meaning in life, or both." Ameara chuckled, realizing how silly she must sound. "By the end, something special usually happened, something to make them happy or hopeful; of course, there were sad stories, too. Some of the stories about love were sad."

"How so?" This time it was Mosa who spoke.

"Sometimes, there was death. Sometimes the man died, sometimes the woman. Some of them made me cry."

"I can't wait to fall in love," said Gaviene beaming. "It must be wonderful."

"You have quite a bit of growing up to do, little miss." Gailia laughed.

"May be," Gavien said, "but you don't and neither does Azalea. She's already in love."

Azalea's cheeks started to turn red, but she was quick to change the subject. "When have you last written to your friend?" She asked, turning to Ameara.

"Early this morning. I sent him a note of encouragement and asked him to let me hear from him soon. He's on a rather dangerous journey and I'm praying that he stays safe."

"Are you nervous not knowing what he looks like?" asked Gaviene. "I know if I was if I cared about a man, I'd at least want to know he was not ugly."

"Gaviene!" Azalea sounded shocked and not a little annoyed. Ameara thought it was the first time she had ever seen her glare at her little sister.

"It's all right," Ameara said. "That's actually a valid point."

"She has seen him though," Mosa said, her lips forming the slightest bit of a smile. "You've seen him in your dreams. The ones the Father has given you."

"Yes, yes, I have."

"You should not be afraid for him. He is part of the Father's plan, as are you. All things will work together in the end. I have a feeling you'll be seeing your handsome stranger before long." She spoke these words solemnly, as if reciting a sacred text. Her tone made Ameara shiver. Azalea had told her before that Mosa was very seldom wrong in matters such as these. But would she be ready? Would she be ready to meet him?

Chapter Thirty-four:
Letting Go

There he stood, holding his place, that beast of nightmares past and present. His bristling back arched towards the sky. The creature's eyes burned with brimstone. They smoldered like a fire dead, yet kept alive by some deep, cancerous hate.

Like Cerberus, he barred the way; blocking the road and any chance of escape. The wolf had only one head, but this was all he needed. He was not a legend or fabled myth, he was real; and he was hungry.

Gillean could hear the rumble of the creature's belly. It grumbled and churned like the workings of a massive furnace. What carnage, what endless death could ever subdue that ravenous flame? Gillean was convinced that when all the hapless inhabitants of the world had been consumed, the beast's hunger would still not be sated. If permitted, it would rend apart the very earth, and after that, the firmament. There was no stopping it, at least, not without aid from the Father.

Gillean set his sights on the monster. He kept his gun leveled at the creature's enormous head. At the same time, there was a restless whisper in his mind.

"You know you've wanted this, an ending sure and complete. Why fight it? Death has eluded you for too long, Gillean. Your end is fixed. Why should it matter how you die? Come, taste the teeth of an old friend. There is nothing left for you here."

The great wolf took a lumbering step forward. Its eyes bore down on him, and its blood-red teeth flashed and glistened of their own accord.

Gillean knew this was not how it was supposed to end. He had been given a promise, and those given by the Father were faithful and true. He felt sweat beading on his forehead and beginning to trickle down his neck. He felt the gnaw of fear, yet stood his ground. *For I know upon whom I have believed and am persuaded that he is able to keep that which I have committed unto him against that day.*

He remembered what he had committed, that which he could not keep hold of himself. Not just his soul, but the very essence of his life, the aspects which made him who he was. The Father Himself was faithful, faithful and true; and he was strong, much stronger than this dark devourer. Despite the state of their fallen world, life would always end up surpassing death; and the giver of life could not be outdone by those who consumed it.

Remembering what he had glimpsed in the vision, Gillean realized his old revolver would not do him much good. Always before, it seemed to help to have something between him and a life-threatening adversary; yet, this time, it did not. His bullets would not pierce that hairy hide, and the beast knew this. It did not rush upon him. The monster was taking his time, toying with his perceived anxiety, attempting to draw him into making the first move.

    Once again, Gillean began to pray. He focused his thoughts and pleas, directing them upward. His faith did not feel strong, yet, he knew that his feelings mattered little. The nagging whispers of discouragement tried again to cloud his thoughts, but he shut then out. If he was to die, he would fall with the truth firmly rooted in his mind.

    All at once, he could see past the terror. He saw the road leading out of town, and Mathias standing upon it, looking back at him. At first, Gillean was not a little perturbed. His life was in peril and all his companion could do was watch. Yet then he understood. Mathias had gained the right to pass before him. He had been weighed and found unwanting. Every man must face the devourer for himself. None might intervene; except by petitioning the Father, that was. He could sense the prayers of his friend and master. They were strong, powerful, availing much. Yet, if he was to pass from this place alive, it would be according to his choice.

In the space of a shattered breath, Gillean realized what he must do. Lowering the revolver, he remembered its former owner, his late wife. It was not the last time he would recall her face, yet it was the last time he would do so with fondness or love. Some things had to be let go.

The moment the revolver fell from his hand, he felt his heart rise up, as if a terrible weight had been removed. A moment later, his knife followed it, accompanied by his heavy pack. The only thing he took from it was the Word of the Father. This he held with steady hand, never even looking down at what he had given up.

He stood, staring down the snarling, beast, weaponless and finally unafraid. He would not fight for himself this day, yet, that did not matter. His God would be his protector.

The monster continued to glare at Gillean. Its frame tensed as if to spring, but it never did. Instead it took a step back. The light of redish-orange flame was waning. The night was falling, yet the natural darkness held a form of brightness all its own. The clouds had vanished and the stars were shinning, clear and strangely close.

Just then, there came a new sound. A low clucking from the alley to his right. Suddenly, a familiar, feathered form trotted into view. It was Char'gabble, the roving rooster. Somehow, he had found his way down from the hills and into this distorted place. The plucky bird shuffled and seemed to eye him with a disdainful gaze then turned towards the devourer. The little rooster flapped his wings and gave the large wolf a low gargling growl then leaped away, cackling. The beast, apparently as surprised as Gillean, snarled and took off after him.

Other than a momentary pang of concern for his pet, Gillean's mind was freed. He rushed forward, leaving his weapons in the dust, and making for the edge of town. There were sounds rising up from behind, echoes of the past, but he heeded them not. His path lay ahead. Mathias was waiting for him.

Chapter Thirty-Five:

Avira's Song

For Gillean, leaving the haunted town behind was like breathing with new lungs. When he finally caught up to Mathias, he was battling a slew of mixed emotions. Part of him wanted to embrace his master and thank him for his prayers. Another part wanted to strike him across the jaw for abandoning him in that awful place. Thankfully, Mathias's air of profound calmness stilled Gillean's soul; and he was content to walk beside him once again. However, he had his share of questions and did not hesitate to ask.

Mathias seemed not to notice that Gillean no longer had the pack and that he was unarmed. He had believed Gillean was following directly behind him. It was only when he had reached the edge of town that he had turned and realized Gillean was gone. He had wanted to turn back, but leaving him to fend for himself had never been his intention. Yet, he had been commanded to continue on; at least until he had crossed the invisible line which separated Klideburn from the rest of the world, the line of demarcation he called it. Gillean admitted that he had understood. It had been his time, his turn to face the devourer once more.

"I know you've encountered him before," said Mathias, a hard smile twisting the corners of his mouth, "but this time, you were grounded in the Father, and he showed you what to do. You were able to let go of what you valued. That is what kills most people. They can never bring themselves to relinquish the things that give them meaning. The beast is going to take them any way."

"Does that include people?" The ones we love, yet cling to, to try and protect."

"No one is ever really safe in our own hands. We have to learn to give those people to God. They were his to begin with." He scratched the back of his neck and looked up at the sky, as if considering what lay beyond the clouds.

"That demon thought he had you. He thought you were an easy kill. He intended to maul you and leave you for dead as before, as he did when Cora betrayed you. Perhaps, Hector intended for him to end you this time. I, for one, am glad the Father allows rematches. We were never supposed to fear creatures like that. They were meant to fear us, to cower at our rebuke and to flee away at our approach. We were meant to be in dominion over them, but that was dependent upon our connection to God."

"Are we not connected to Him even now?"

"Aye, that we are; but not fully, not as we should be, not one hundred percent of the time. We need to draw closer." He eyed the black, bound tome in Gillean's hand.

"We will need to do some reading before we go up against what lies at the end of our road. Reading and praying. Not only our lives, but our purpose may depend on it."

"Even if we are in perfect relation, perfect sync with His Word and heart, We'll need him to fight with us and for us. I can't claim credit for anything that happened back there. If He had not helped me, I don't know if I would have been able to hold my mind together. That thing, the devourer, it has a way of attacking you on the inside."

"Perhaps more viciously than any physical assault," Mathias agreed.

"Even when I dropped the pack and my weapons, I wasn't sure if I would be allowed to walk away. I'm just so thankful that God sent Char'gabble when he did."

Mathias turned back to him, a keen glint in his eye. The look surprised Gillean. It stung of suspicion. Had his honesty been called into question. Gillean felt a flicker of anger begin to rise in his chest, yet quickly strove to extinguish it. Even if his words had kindled some form of mistrust, becoming defiant and losing his cool would do nothing to remedy this. He realized also that his nerves were shot. His ordeal had left him shaken and quite possibly a bit confused. He took in a deep breath and attempted to clear his head.

"What exactly happened before you walked away?"

"I know it sounds crazy, but it was Char'gabble. I'd know that rooster anywhere. He's the one I told you about. He must have come looking for me. He hopped out into the street as casual as you please. He didn't even seem frightened. The wolf just took off after him."

"I believe you," said Mathias as if sensing his feelings, "yet, does not this seem strange? It is peculiar, is it not? Why should a creature like that chase a bird? Why would a monstrous demon of worlds past which has consumed more than we will ever know, pursue a common, barnyard chicken? The Devourer's hunger is not merely for flesh as you well know. It craves destruction."

Gillean was liking the look in his master's eyes less and less. Clearly, Mathias sensed something else behind this, some encircling vibe, some feeling of latent misgiving. He wished Mathias would just speak plainly and be done with it, all the mystery and subtle apprehension. This quest and its approaching end were already more cryptic enough for his liking.

"When you put it that way, it does sound a little more than odd. Do you think it was all a ruse, a trick to throw us off our guard?"

"It would not be the first time," Mathias said slowly. "They call Hector the deceiver for good reason. His executions of this craft are many and varied. He is cunning and skillful in his dark arts. Don't think he doesn't know who you are and what you desire. In some ways, he knows us better than we know ourselves."

They kept on walking beneath the star-strewn sky. The moon's glowing was faint, yet, the crystal dots surrounding it shown vibrantly. The road was clear, vacant of life and leavings. Gillean kept expecting to see some old cart or vehicle resembling the one they had "borrowed" at Gaven post. He was not quite sure why his mind wished to associate this winding stretch with those old, outdated machines. It had been years, centuries since they had been widely used. Most likely, this road had never seen one. Their rumbling, shuddering engines had long since been replaced by the more efficient air-ships and hover-craft; which, in their turn had become rare following the wars. It was a curious thing, the progression of man's devices. Just when he thought he had found the way, the key to sustain and remain; his efforts were cast down, most often violently. What was the lesson? What was this world, or God, trying to teach them? Finality? Futility? Somehow, it did not seem to matter. What was, was; and what had been was passed away. Their world was dying, quite possibly, for the final time. Its days had been prenumbered, and had nearly run their course.

They were both growing weary, yet neither of them wanted to stop until Klideburn was further behind them. They would make camp soon, yet neither reckoned they would sleep much anyway, not after the day they had had. It would be well if they could only close their eyes for a few hours.

The land had changed once again. It rose up on either side of the road in terraced steps. Lines of tangled vines stretched like wings in the moon-light, the remnants of a vineyard. Looking closely, Gillean thought he saw new growth beginning to lace amongst the trellises. How could this be? His heart leapt with excitement as he considered it. Maybe there was some life left in this world after all.

As they went higher, the terraces merged into tree-covered slopes. Sycamore and alder interlaced their boughs and willows hung their heads as if in grief. Mathias breathed out. The sound was sudden, but soft as a gentle wind. Gillean was about to ask if he was all right, yet the words never left his lips. Suddenly, he too realized the miracle surrounding them. Everything was alive. Not just the trees, but the slopes themselves. They held a warmth, a living, breathing glow. Not one which could be seen, but one which was impossible not to feel. The very ground seemed to pulse with it, like the stir and beating of some enormous heart.

They both stopped in their tracks. Gillean wanted to speak, but he dared not. There was something about this place which held their very thoughts in check. Suddenly, he knew; this ground was holy.

In silence, both men removed their boots in a gesture of respect; one which had almost been forgotten in this world. The thrumming ground felt light beneath his feet. There was a restfulness here, a peace which surpassed anything they could ever think or feel. He hoped it would continue on with them.

They must have looked a strange sight, those two men, standing in their tattered sock feet, drinking in the cool night air. To the world, they would have seemed like fools, but they would not have cared. What they did, they did to honor God, and the blessing He had poured out upon this place; this quiet corner in the hills, this pocket of enduring life.

From beyond their scope of vision came a voice; soft and fragile, yet braded with an underlying strength. It was singing: singing words of a long-forgotten song. Gillean recognized it instantly, and he could feel his spirit sore at the sound. His heart sought to cry out, to join in; and in doing so, give voice to its deepest self. As the singer drew near, it did. They both sang, boldly, without shame or second thought. This was a song from the Father.

> "Can you tell of all the wonders of His earth,
> Of the breath and color whispered on the winds?
> What is life that bones should grow within the womb?
> What is man that thou should take a thought for him?
> Tell of the treasures of his might,
> Of the soul-cheering voice of his heart.
> There are none who walk in sacred love
> Without God's glorious light.
> The golden skies and the joyous dawns,
> All the sweetness that our eyes do drink,
> For a living breath we shall lift our song,
> Give all praises to the sovereign King.
> For the petals that fly on the wings of the wind,
> From the fires that take and the waters which give,
> May we see and receive all thy blessings bestowed,
> May we breathe as the trees as we live out our thread.
> Can you tell of the wonders of He who enfolds
> Every creature and heart in his infinite arms.

When the storms fly upon you, be still and rejoice,
For a peace with his presence He gives.
Take delight in the ways he has fashioned the earth,
In the lines and the loveliness free.
Give song and remember, these days shall not die.
They are stored up in Heaven for thee."

As they continue to sing, the one who began the song approaches. She is a woman in her late forties, though her troubled years have made her seem much older. Her hair is ashen gray and she is smiling; yet within, she holds a sadness too deep and sorrowful for words. Her name is Amira, weaver of cloth, and a teller of stories.

Since the day her children were taken by the Assembly, she has waited to be reunited with them. She believes that God has promised her this. She believes that, before she dies, they will be together again. She holds to hope, yet the bitter years have takin a toll on her heart. These days, it is all she can do to sing the songs of her Father and keep her hope alive.

The stories which she tells are beautiful and lifelike, though most times sad. People come from miles around to hear them. Some say, these tales are more than what they seem. It is believed by some that they are visions, either of what has happened or what is to come. Avira has very much doubted this, until recently, that is.

Avira has had vison, a story set within her mind. It was the tale of a man, a servant who would wander the wastelands, eventually to arrive at her village. He would be following behind a holy man.

This man was a mighty warrior, though he knew it not. It was he who would face the evil arising from the east. It was he who, with the strength of the Father, would fight against the dark monsters attempting to consume their world.

Avira does not know when he shall arrive, only that he will. There is something which she must give to him, a chest of rosewood. It was given to her husband long ago by a mysterious man. A man who called himself Gordon Vordebt.

When the two travelers catch sight of her, Avira stops. She smiles at them. Their singing falls silent. They seem concerned, yet not fearful. Instantly, she knows who they are.

"Welcome, Gillean Weaver and Mathias St. john. You have come far. I am Avira Theorah. I've been waiting for you."

Mathias seemed withdrawn, perhaps a little apprehensive; yet Gillean could tell right away that this woman was sent of the Father. The still, small voice spoke clear. Here was one whom they could trust.

"Good evening," said Gillean, bowing. He was not quite sure why he did this. It was as if her presence required. It. "You seem to know our names, do you know of our quest?"

"Indeed, I do. I have been waiting many years for what you will accomplish. I feared that you might be delayed.

"We were," spoke Mathias. The sudden warmth in his tone surprised Gillean. "Yet, we have come all the same. Tell me, good woman, how far is it to the gates, the place they call Akron?"

"That name is both feared and hated in these parts, but I am glad that you speak it with courage. It is not far, about twenty miles south east, as the crow flies. Your journey is nearly done, but you must take rest before its final leg. Come with me and you will have a place to rest, as well as a meal. The Father has instructed me to see you are tended to."

"Thank you," said Mathias. "We shall go with you. May the will of the Father bless and keep you all your days."

So, they followed her, leaving the winding road behind them. After some short distance, they stopped to put their boots back on. The resonance of holy ground still tingled against their feet, yet it was only an echo. As they moved through the hills towards the valley beyond, it faded and was gone as swiftly as if had come.

Below them, rolling pasture lands swelled out like the bowl of a sloping wave. In the window of a small, white cottage, a candle was burning. Its light guided them in; and soon, they found themselves at rest beside a wide and roaring fire.

Chapter Thirty-six:
The Pale Queen

The mountain winds cut hard against the stone as another storm closed in. Beyond the gates of Akron, the forbidden city of Arius stood as dark and sullen as it has since the beginning. Its domes and towers were sentinels, watchers of the advancing walls of cloud. No light burned within their windows. None was needed. Those who dwelt there could see better in the dark.

At the southern edge of the city, not far from the narrow pass, stood a facility. Unlike the rest of the buildings, its walls were white. They were high and pointed, surrounded by pillars. Outside in the blustery wind, armored guards, Mavarians, hung about waiting for their orders.

The dirt-bare yard was filled with holes, some small, some large. Most were shallow, about six to eight feet in diameter. The largest were encircled with slanted poles laced about with strands of wire. They pulsed and shimmered, their thin lines glowing in hues of blue and purple, indwelt by restless, burning current.

As the black storm clouds clustered above, a door opened. It moved on soundless hinges, swinging wide, powered by some hidden energy. The Mavarian guards stood to attention. They watched as the students marched forth in double rows. These were the children of Arius, now young adults. These were the chosen ones, stolen from their parents in the dead of night. They had met every requirement, learning the ways of the Sacred Assembly and submitting themselves fully to its god. It was they who would carry on the dominion. It was they who would advance from this failing world into the mystery which lay beyond.

They were dressed in black. Their robes, woven in the high citadel, bore the insignia of the laurel-wreathed A. Their faces were vacant, devoid of expression or emotion. All natural affection had been purged from their minds. They were unburdened by conscience or compassion. The ideal warriors for the new dark age.

As the Mavarians hissed and clucked, the youth were led towards the shallow pits. Gates were opened in the wire and the first four dozen were ushered into the pits. There was a crackling sound, and the air came alive with the smell of ozone. The grotesque guards cackled as the clouds above began to churn. With a sudden burst of energy, purple flares of lightening struck down from the storm. They danced about the wires, it encircled those inside, illuminating their vacant faces. Somewhere, a dial was turned, and the flares intensified. The white-hot heat rippled the air. Suddenly, with a pulse of dirty light, the youth were gone.

As a new group issued forth, a woman appeared near the largest of the craters. She was tall, with dark eyes and skin as pale as chalk. There seemed to be no life in her, yet she moved like one indwelt with supernatural strength. The aura of her chilling countenance filled the air, and it was enough to make the guards immediately take notice.

The Mavarian leading the new group, a thin man with the head of a lizard, stopped in his tracks, a look of perplexed fear upon his face. The pale woman eyed him with a malevolent gaze. Her jet-black eyes flickered slightly, and he knew he was in deep trouble. When she spoke, it was as an echo. It seemed to come from somewhere deep beneath the earth.

"And what, pray tell, are you doing?"

"Your majesty, forgive me...I am, we are transporting these to the out-post. They are ready to serve."

The woman's gaze did not change. "No."

"Your majesty?" The Mavarian was shaking now.

"They have not yet been initiated. There minds are not ready."

The lizard man was speechless. He cowered before her, knowing what was to come. From deep within his throat came a low gurgling moan.

The pale woman snapped her fingers and the creature's skull was broken. He fell back in a heap, falling to ash in the twinkling of an eye. The students, unmoved at the man's fate, stared blankly ahead. At a motion from her, they turned and headed back towards the white building. They would be content to wait. The queen knew best. It was she who had been mother to them all.

Watching them go, Keres Leah smiled inwardly. This world might be ending, yet the future had never been so full of promise. There were many worlds, each with its own unique shape and structure. Disorder abounded, yet, with the guidance of her master, they would bring them all into unity. And what of the Father, that mighty one who surveyed their work with judging eye? Well, what of Him? He would surely meet his end just as all the gods. Nothing man worshiped was immortal. Once they had all creation in their grasp, they would turn their attention to Him.

As she stood, transfixed by her dark thoughts, a shadow crept up beside her. Keres looked down and smiled. The tamandua stared back at her. his obsidian eyes were so much like her own, soft and doleful in the dimming light.

"Is all well?" She asked. "Are the others in place?"

"Yes, my queen. All is ready for the morrow. It shall be a wonder such as none have ever seen."

"Very good, Penteros. It shall be well. The minds of men are weak. They shall fold unto our purpose like molten glass. You shall have your worshipers, and I- I shall have my kingdom, just as Hector promised."

Penteros, whose name really was something else entirely, smiled to himself. *Oh, you shall have your kingdom, lady. It shall be an eternal kingdom, one of flames and endless suffering. There you shall languish by our side forever.*

The evil beast knew there was no hope for them, he knew this better than any. Yet, hope was never his goal. It had always been destruction, and the subversion of men's souls unto the way of everlasting death.

Chapter Thirty-seven:
A Seething Pot

A seething pot set upon a livid flame, a rider in dark raiment galloping away, a toothy maw poised to swallow up the world; these were the images which Gillean saw within his dreams. Even before he woke, he wanted to disown them. He wanted to believe that they meant nothing, and that they had no bearing on what was soon to unfold. Yet, he knew better. In its current state, dreams were as much a part of this world as anything else.

When he awoke, it was early morning. After building up the fire in the hearth, he was able to read some of the Father's word and pen a short note to the woman with whom he had been corresponding. She called herself Ameara now. Gillean did not fully understand the reasons behind her change of name, yet he felt she was still the lovely woman of his dreams, now more than ever. Even from another world, her heart called to his. He could feel it. It was a burning, deep and sure, a warmth he carried with him, even on the coldest of nights. He longed to see her, to speak to her face to face. Strange as it seemed, he felt he loved her. It was not rational; yet, If it was the will of the Father, man's reasoning would have little to do with it.

As he helped their host with the morning chores, he wondered about Mathias. His friend and master was still asleep. He had been weary and needed rest, but there was something else, some murky presence had leveled itself over his persona. Gillean had first noticed the change after they left Klideburn. It had taken over his whole affect. Yes, he had become more somber since his experience on the road, the night he had saved him from Lillith; yet his soul seemed burdened now, as if he was trying to hold back some sinister weight.

"Do you believe your master has a word from the Lord?" Avira spoke as if sensing his thoughts.

"I don't know. If he has, he hasn't told me."

"Do you believe he's a true prophet?" Gillean could sense he was being tested and he didn't much like it. "Not all prophets speak openly. Besides, it may not be time for him to speak. God has given him a purpose, and I am honored to stand with him."

"What do you expect to find at the gates?"

"The enemies of humanity, most likely. I know not how we'll face them, yet, it is as God has said. He has not called the equipped; He equips the called."

"Take heart, Gillean. You are stronger than you believe. What you have gone through has made you so. The Father is faithful and true. He will not give you anything more than you can bear."

"What do you know of my life?" Gillean was a little angry, yet more surprised than anything else.

"I know enough. The Spirit speaks expressly concerning you, and the Father has shared with me at least a portion your story."

From inside the cottage, a tea kettle began to whistle, and the smell of fresh bread wafted through the window. It was a relaxing scent, mixed with aromas of lilac and camphor. It smelled like home.

"Come. There it is time for breakfast. And there is something that I have to show you. You may have need of it if you intend to face the gates of Akron."

Once back inside, Avira went to her stove. She removed the kettle, and took the bread from the oven. It smelled even more wonderful than it had from the yard.

Gillean went over to where Mathias was lying. The weary prophet had turned to face the wall and his cloak and blanket were pulled up, covering his head. Gillean touched his shoulder, and started to speak, but the words caught in his throat. Despite the warmth of the fire and his many wrappings, his friend and master was cold. In the kitchen, Avira had ceased her movements.

Gillean's breath caught in his throat. Slowly, fearfully, he turned the man over and lifted the hood of his cloak. Somewhere deep inside his chest, an obscure flame flickered, dimmed, and went out. Mathias St. John, his beloved friend and companion, was dead.

Chapter Thirty-eight:
The Letter and the Chest

"No! Oh no." Gillean fell back and pressed the tips of his fingers into his eyes. How could Mathias be dead. He just couldn't be, not now. Not on the verge of the most critical leg of their journey.

Gillian had felt that in many ways, this was his master's quest. He was thankful for the purpose he had been provided, to be able to serve and aid where he was needed. Yet, he had not been the one to receive direction as to where they should go. He had depended upon Mathias for that. Without his friend and master, he felt blind.

After surviving alone for so long, Gillean had been slow to trust this man; yet once he had, their bond had grown strong. Now, sitting beside his mentor's lifeless corpse, all the things Mathias had taught him came flooding back to mind. The man had proven a constant encouragement, a strength to his faith. When their situation was darkest, or seemed insurmountable, he had always found the words to keep them strong. Unlike Gillean, his focus had always been fixed upon the Father. Gillean could truly say he had never known a more devout nor selfless man of God. He was the only friend he had left. And now, he was gone; stolen away in the dead of night. Oh, the bitter wrongness of it all. By rights, it should have been he, Gillean, who was not allowed to continue.

Avira knelt beside him on the floor. Her eyes were sad and her voice was soft as she spoke. "It's not your fault. We can never know when our souls will be required of us. They are only on loan after all."

Gillean's heart, which was still seared and seething, wanted him to lash out, to rebuke this woman and her seemingly knowing words. Yet, his spirit told him that she was right. As long as the Father had willed it, Mathias had lived; and nothing, truly nothing could have ended him. Yet, when the Father calls home a soul, who can prevent it or say Him nay. Gillean could not comprehend why Mathia's time had come, perhaps he never would; yet there it was, the will of the Father, cutting into him like a knife.

He nodded slowly, trying to hold back tears. "What you say is true. I suppose we should be thankful that he passed in peace."

He looked upon the cold face, its lips colorless, its cheeks sunken in death. "I can accept this. I don't want to, but I can. I know he's at peace. I just wish he hadn't left. It sort of puts a cramp in our plans. Whatever we were headed forth to face, I don't believe it was meant to he confronted alone. Now, I don't, I don't know what I can do."

"You must continue. You must." Avira's voice was thin, yet forceful, almost desperate. "You cannot turn back now. The Father led you here for a purpose. He chose you, Gillean. You are His appointed champion."

Even as she spoke, there was a stirring in his heart. His inner voice (that of his soul) which had wanted to cry out in desperation and question the Father, had now been quelled. It had given way to another, the still small admonition which had for so long sustained his steps. He would see this venture through, even unto death. Gillean would confront the evil and challenge it head on. He would fight in the name of the Father. He would do it for his friend, whose final breaths had been devoted to singing the praises of Almighty God. He would do it for the stolen children, those ushered through the cursed pass of Akron, to the fearful city beyond. And lastly, he would do it for himself. He would strike a blow against the Assembly and their great and grievous lies. Gillean was positive they were a core part of this abomination, this horrendous four personed god of which he had been told. If he was not of their device or creation, they were at least complicit as servants of the one called Hector. Gillean had no doubt that he would be at Akron too, in some form at least. This was it, the long-awaited chance to face his chiefest foe; and God willing, repay him for all which he had taken. If he was given a chance, just one chance, he would strike the devil down. It would be his most fervent endeavor; for with the fall of Hector, what other wrongs might be extinguished, stricken from the earth? Slaying him might not save this blighted world, yet it would be a start.

"Steel your mind!" Avira cried, sensing his thoughts. "Look unto the Father, not to the hope of vengeance. Be driven by His purpose, but not consumed with anger. The Devourer waits for such as fall from focus. Don't make yourself an easy prey. As for facing the enemy alone, you need not fear. I shall go with you and so shall the people of my village. There are many who have suffered at the hand of the evil directly, even more who would stand against it. Yes, we may all be destroyed, yet not in full. As long as our souls are secure, belonging to the Father, what lies ahead can never truly harm us. Remember that and you will have no true reason for fear."

Gillean agreed. It was a lot to take in all at once, yet he had no choice. This was here and now, and there was little time for reflection. Soon he would be going to battle and he would need all the help he could get.

Suddenly, the rest of the blanket covering Mathias's arm fell away, and Gillean could see that he had been clutching a crinkled envelope. Carefully, he took hold of it and slipped it from his grasp. It was addressed to Gillean and bore the following instructions.

These are the words I have been given. Take them, heed them, make use of them as you will; yet do not open and read them until thy current task is completed. Stand against the evil, Gillean, stand and be not dismayed. The Father is with thee.

Gillean took the last words passed to him by his friend and master, and tucked them into his pocket. As much as he wanted to read them, he decided to honor Mathias's request. If he survived, perhaps he could take some comfort in them. It would be something to look forward to.

As Gillean covered Mathias with the blanket, he looked over at his host. She had risen and was rummaging around in a corner closet. In a moment she emerged, haulling something heavy. Gillean moved to help her, and together, they pulled the object into the center of the room. It was a chest, at least three feet long and three feet wide, made from rose wood. Its dark and rusty hue glowed in the fire-light. When it was opened, the smell of sawdust and sweet oil filled Gillean's nostrils. Its contents were as follows: two daggers, each fitted with a black wood, grooved handle: a short sword, curved and sharpened to a razor's edge, two leather pouches filled with ten -millimeter shells, a leather cross bandolier, and four gray, long-barreled revolvers. The guns were crafter by hand, fashioned by some workman who had long since left to meet his maker. Each well-fit cylinder held seven shells. Their hammers were sleek with wide, thumb-shaped backs. They were all double action, built for swift shooting and heated battles.

"I have rifles and scatter-guns if you prefer those, but these were left especially for you."

"Left? Left by whom?"

"A man brought them here years ago. I think you might know him. His name was Gordon, Gordan Vordebt."

Chapter Thirty-nine:
For Such a Time as This

"Is Gordon alive?" Gillean asked, his expression suddenly hopeful.

"I don't know for certain," Avira began, but then she paused, seeming to consider. A far-off look overtook her eyes, and her lips moved involuntarily.

"Something tells me he is," she continued. "I feel he may yet have a part to play in the lives of many. Not in this world, mayhaps, but somewhere, he may cross your path again. If he does, listen to him. Take heed to his words and what he would say, for he is wise. He would have spared you much suffering in your life had Hector not succeeded in silencing him, temporarily at least. You may not have always realized this, but he loved you like a brother, Gillean. His prayers for you have never ceased, even when your faith faltered and became weak. It is the Spirit of the Father who has told me this, so I know that it is true."

Gillean had many a question, yet he decided these could wait. Just believing that his oldest friend still lived and was looking out for him made all the difference in the world.

They had fought together in the first battle of the last war, when the Sons of Veritas had endeavored to throw off the yoke of the Assembly.

Gillean had flown with Gordan in his armored airship, raining down a barrage of fire upon the enemy troops. Gordon had tried to destroy Gillean's wife, Cora, who had fought against them under the influence of Hector. Even though she was trying to kill them, Gillean had not wanted this, yet he understood why his friend had done what he did. Cora had become a witch; and dark powers, though barrowed, had threatened to burn away everything for which they had worked.

    Now, years later, it all felt like a dream; a memory from a forgotten age, a part of someone else's life. After his craft had been shot down, Gordon Vordebt had vanished. Everyone who knew him said that he was dead. His loss was felt and mourned all throughout the forces of the rebellion. They had held a vigil for him with candles, and the pomp deemed befitting. The Sons of Veritas hailed him as a hero, a martyr for the cause, and they pledged that his death would be avenged. Gillean had parted ways from them after this. He hadn't trusted the new leadership. They were reckless, volatile, driven by hate and other equally unstable emotions. For the most part, this was why they had lost. It had ceased to be about the common people and had become a vendetta. This was a lesson which Gillean should have remembered. Had he done so, the next few days might have had a very different outcome.

To Gillean, Gordon Vordebt's disappearance had never made sense. True, he could have been flung from the wreckage as was commonly believed. Yet, as he had once written in his journal, that explanation just didn't feel right. Whatever the case, Gillean had never really abandoned the hope that he would see his old friend again. And now, here it was, the proof that Gordan had been looking out for him as directed by the Father; and evidence that he might still be breathing.

Gillean had very little appetite, yet Avira encouraged him to eat of what she had prepared. It felt wrong, most irreverent to be stuffing his face with his dead companion lying cold beside the hearth. Still, Gillean did just that. He knew he had to if he was to continue on. It had been quite some time since he had taken any nourishment. Food was not a big deal for him these days. Most times it barely mattered at all. Hunger pains would dull and dissipate when ignored for long enough. To his shame, he could still remember a time when food had been a primary motivator; when a missed meal left him feeling weak, irritable like a cranky child. In many ways, he had been a child, a foolish one. That was one good thing the hardships in his life had done; the breaking of his selfish nature. It had been a hard lesson to learn, but to fully abound in the Spirit, he first had to be abased, trampled upon until He could learn to depend more deeply upon the Father.

Man shall not live on bread alone, he thought as he slowly chewed, *But by every word that proceeds from the mouth of God.*

While he finished his meal, Avira had left the cottage. She had gone to gather the people of her village. Doubtless, there would be some skeptics (skepticism abounded in these perilous times) yet, the word of the storyteller was well respected here. The majority of them would heed her call and would follow her to the gates of Hell if they were asked. They would eagerly prepare for war.

Gillean had wished to burry Mathias. He felt it was the least he could do for his departed master. Yet Avira had told him to let the body lie where it was, at least for now.

"We will tend to him and lay him to rest. There are certain old men among us who shall see to that. Undertakers we call them. You need to retain all your strength. Look over your new weapons, familiarize yourself with them. You were called; now, you have been equipped. When the people come, they will expect to see you armed and ready. It is you who shall lead us to the gates."

And the Father will be leading me, he thought as he rose from the table.

Gillean stepped over to the rosewood chest. He surveyed each item once again, carefully considering its use. He held the weapons up, examining them in the light from the window. He tested the weight and balance of the blades, and the ergonomics of the guns. Gillean was sure he would find some flaw in them, no matter how slight, yet, he did not. Aside from being a tad bulky, they were perfect. Their long, grooved barrels slid effortlessly into his belt had held secure. Two he tucked in back, the other two in front; the dark and crimson grips facing each other like foreboding bookends. They were the color of blood. Not man's blood, but that of his enemy. A reflection of that which he would soon be spilling.

As he gazed upon them, the fire inside rekindled; yet his eyes became cold and hard as steel ice. He thought back to the valley of children's bones, to the town of Klideburn, left desolate by the great, demonic wolf; and he thought of a certain creature perched atop the pulpit of an old and dusty church. Those demons, how dare they subvert the sacred? How dare they strive to exalt themselves against the very fabric of nature, imposing with impunity the purest of God's gifts. They would all surely burn, yet before they did, they would find themselves thrown into the struggle of their lives. They and all those in league with them would taste the wrath of the Father. His instruments and implements had been sharpened, honed unto a razor's edge. The Father Himself had laid them out and had polished them for just such a time as this: a day of violence and garments rolled in blood.

Chapter Forty:
Ameara's Plea

Ameara was walking through a place she had never been; a field cloaked in dimming light. The wiry stems of peculiar plants swayed and bobbed. There was no wind, yet, their movements were constant and unchanged. Ahead of her, a cluster of black and thorny trees rose up against the fading sky. It was growing darker with every passing minute, yet it was not twilight; the dimness felt more permanent than that.

This is a dream, she thought to herself. *I am having a dream, and if I don't like it, I can just wake myself up.*

Indeed, she wanted to wake up. This place was eerie, and the more her eyes took in, the less she liked it. The field in which she stood felt like a graveyard, a cemetery which had yet to be. It was a place of impending death in which life could not remain for long. Yet, try as she might, she could not pull herself from sleep. Her feet kept her moving forward, the direction she least wanted to go. Unwillingly, she was drawn towards the barbed and tangled wood.

Ameara could hear voices. They were chanting in unison. Some kind of sing-song rhythm bound them together, as if they too were captives of this despondent place. There was harmony, yet also discord, like a piano whose wires are loose and rusted.

Reaching the raven-colored sprawl of thorny brush, she peered through to see a ghastly sight. The worshipers numbered in the thousands. They gathered like flies, and quivering like quail. They were like the plants; some swaying, some bowing, all with their eyes fixed upon the flames and the colossal terror which towered above them.

The beasts were enormous; massive, lizard-like monsters, called forth from some forgotten corner of Hell itself. They were black, as black as the trees. Their reptilian eyes flashed and narrowed against the flames. Those eyes were familiar. They burned with a slow and putrid flame, smoldering with poisoned red. She felt if she looked on them too long, her very heart would sour and die. Even with her gaze averted, Ameara knew she had seen those eyes before, yet she could not recall where. Thankfully, the grace of the Father had barred the memory from her mind.

It was then that she realized, these grotesque creatures were connected. Their thick, scaled tails were bound by an overlying flap of skin. It crinkled and curved as they moved, like the folded wing of a dead bat.

Suddenly, these horrid creatures merged completely, becoming as one. Their teeth and eyes drew together in a jumble, a mockery of any created thing they might have once resembled. Ameara sensed the spirits of the beasts were residing individually within the titan. She did not know how she knew this, yet it seemed like a logical assumption. They were each concealed, tucked away within the massive frame. The creature made her feel small, worthless, and oh so bitterly alone. As she looked upon its eyes once again, it was as if the whole world had died and was decaying around her. The other people were as wraiths. She was the last whisper of the Father's light; a single, solitary flower in a field possessed by darkness.

    The crowds, wether dead or living, were oblivious to her. They worshiped the beast, calling out and praying to it in their humming, nasal, song-like tones. Ameara wondered how the thing could have such a hold on them. She had the feeling that it had been given great power and authority. Authority from whom? Not the Father, surely. Could it be...the Unicorn?

    The name was confusion to her; the thought most entirely bizarre. Why had this word, this notion popped into her mind? Unicorns were the stuff of children's stories, usually good, she thought. Besides, they were not real. The holy church had always insisted that they were not, and that had always been good enough for her. Yet, in a world where such a terror might live and breathe, she supposed anything was possible. This thing, it was far too hideous and unspeakably evil to simply be a dream. This was a nightmare. A nightmare which she most ardently desired to depart from.

As the beginnings of a prayer toucher her lips, something compelled her to turn around. Ameara did, and for an instant, completely forgot the awful monster and its corrupting eyes. There, striding across the shadowed field, was Gillean, the man for which she had been waiting.

Without a second thought, she ran to him. There was an aura about him, a glow of light so intense she could not resist. She wanted to be near him, to feel his strong and caring arms around her.

He looked up and saw her. His face broadened in to a smile. He flung wide his arms and they embraced each other. His shirt and vest smelled of honey, and leather. She lifted her eyes to his and their gazes intertwined. The pure, perfect blue of hers seemed reflected in the soft and graying blue of his. In many ways, their faces were very much alike; hers softer and narrower, ye still matching the arch of his brow and the slope of his chin and nose. It was a sweet face, kind and beautiful, she thought. It was one that she could trust.

"Gillean. You finally found me! I knew you would. I knew the Father would lead you aright. After everything we've come through, at last, we can be together. You don't know how I've longed for this day."

"I too," He replied, the warmth of his voice caressing her heart. "For countless days and endless nights, I have longed for you, to see your face, and hear your voice, but most of all to feel your wonderous heart beating against my own. You have inspired me, my darling Amanda. Your love has given me the strength I needed to carry on."

"My name is Ameara now, my sweet. The Father re-named me when he saved me from the sea. He named be after a flower which grows in Heaven."

Gillean was silent at this, yet his silence did not trouble her in the least. His warmth and presence were all she needed. They would talk more later. For now, she wanted simply to treasure the moment.

With glowing satisfaction, she felt her long-awaited love returning her embrace; but then she felt him endeavoring to pry himself away from her. Ameara was shocked and not a little confused. For a moment, she tried to fight his efforts, struggling against them, striving to keep him close. Yet it was all in vain. Gillean broke free from her grasp and proceeded to push past her towards the place beyond the snarling trees where that hideous thing awaited to ensnare men's minds as if they were children.

"No, Gillian!" she shrieked, unafraid of who might hear. "No! That monster is the bringer of destruction, the ender of worlds! We must leave! The Father has a place prepared for us. There is nothing for you here but death and agony! Gillian!"

Slowly, methodically, he turned to look at her; and to her astonished horror, his eyes had changed. They now bore the red and morbid light, the very smoldering evil which indwelt the eyes of monster. It had already begun to affect him.

Ameara gave a stifled cry, as tears streamed down her pale cheeks. She could not lose him now, not like this. She would rather die.

"I love you, Amanda," He said, thoughtlessly using her former name, "But I must do this as the Father has commanded. I must kill the beast."

Chapter Forty-one:
The March

In the early darkness of the morning, the people of the village gathered for their march to Akron. Odaunta was a small community, and most of its inhabitants were up in years; yet, they were all eager to fight, both men and women. Most had scores of their own to settle with the servants of the Assembly. They had lost children and grandchildren, mothers, fathers, brothers, husbands, and wives. All had suffered and been forced to carry on without someone they had loved.

Those ruling over the surviving common people considered them weak. For decades, they had been looked down on as stupid and uncouth, unworthy of what little they managed to possess. The patrols from Arius seldom came this way nowadays; yet when they did, they spat upon the townspeople and took whatever they wanted, not caring if some elderly couple would starve come winter. The delusion that the ruling governmental authority was anointed of God had been abandoned by most. Those who still held loyalty to the "Laurels" had long since been stoned or cast out. Now, with the man called Gillean leading them, they were ready to make their stand.

With those come down from the hills, their force numbered sixty-five in all. There were also about twenty or so elders who would follow along behind to tend to the wounded and render assistance however they could. Avira had sent word to the surrounding communities, and expected several hundred to come to their aid, yet they could not wait for these. God willing, they would meet at the narrow gates. This was the day appointed and the hour of reckoning was drawing nigh.

There were no working air-ships in Odaunta, none of the old vehicles either. Yet, oddly enough, they did have horses. Although the Assembly strictly forbade the private ownership of such animals, this had not stopped the wily men of the hills. They had "rescued" the first of them as foals from a nearby sanctuary and had been breeding them ever since. They kept them in secret, hidden stables, only allowing them out to run at night. There were few flyovers these days, yet their keepers took no chances. Each and every person was well aware of what would happen when they were discovered, yet they seemed not to care. These people took great pride in their horses. They fed them off what little they were able to grow, many times treating them better than their own families.

It saddened Gillean to understand the depths of their sacrifice. Most likely the majority of these noble beasts would be slain this day; most of these people, too. Yet, they were not concerned with this. Most seemed weary of just residing. They had come to accept that death would find them either way. What mattered now was the spirit with which they met their end. For too long had they been denied respect. The Assembly, and the world at large, had thrown them away like filthy rags. The old ways which they loved had been rejected, forgotten amidst a new age of barbarism and depravity. Yet, these old people of Odaunta still remembered. They remembered a world which had once been clean; a place where families had thrived and men and women had been free to live and worship as they chose, as the Father led them. It was for the sake of these recollections that they now rode and walked towards the gates of Akron with Gillean and Avira at their head. They had determined to sell what remained of their lives for them, and for the children taken in the night.

Their armaments were many and varied. Most of the villagers had some type of firearm, be it rifle, pistol, or scatter-gun. Some held bows, with quivers of arrows slung across their shoulders. There were crude spears and axes snatched from the woodpile; ancient blades and rusted farm implements. A very few possessed what Gillean referred to as "rapid-fire weapons." These were older and less accurate than any rifle, yet they could spit bullets as fast as one could tap the trigger. The

Assembly Guard had often used these; and Gillean disliked them, yet, in the approaching fight, they would doubtless prove useful.

As grim daylight rose into the stormy sky, the hills and trees began to fall away. The withered grass became hard-packed earth, rocky and unforgiving. Filaments of copper, chert, and graphite streaked the jutting stones. Here and there, the ruins of a dwelling or some other neglected thing lay littered amongst the wastes.

Off to their left, Gillean could see a cluster of bones. They were strewn across a wide sand-pit, in which the stony ground fell away in a sickening, concave slope. Most of the remains appeared to be human, yet running through their center was an enormous spine; a collection of sallow vertebrae and the beginnings of a colossal ribcage.

Here there were monsters, Gillean thought as he looked away, *And mayhap there still are.*

He tried to pay them no more notice, yet as he rode past, they seemed to call to him, to whisper in low and restless tones. Gillean attempted to steel his mind, to fill it with the praises of the Father, yet the voices followed him. Their pitch rose to a thinning whine, mocking him, scraping against his raw nerves as if to test his sanity.

"Your master lies within the stony ground," they wailed, "soon, and very soon, you shall be joining him. Why throw away your life? This one is all there is. You dream of Heaven, of a merciful God. Have you ever seen such, or even anything to suggest such fanciful things exist? You should not trust in dreams. There is no true reality in them. Gods are for the weak, those who need a crutch to explain away their shortcomings. The churches are gone, Gillean. The prophets and preachers are dead, their bones scattered with our own. Your mind is lost, lost in a sea of shifting sand. Come down from your high horse. Throw yourself at our mercy. Your madness is incurable, by we will let you keep your life. All you must do is throw yourself to us and renounce your delusions."

"In the Father's name, be silent!" Gillean spoke forcefully, not caring that he spoke aloud. The others looked at him with shocked dismay, yet one look from their storyteller kept them silent. Avira turned back to Gillean, a look of steadfast courage in her eyes.

"The gates are not far now. The closer we come, the more the demons will try and hold you back. Be of good courage. Greater is He who is in you than He who resides in this place. Soon, your quest shall be at an end."

"I know you're right," said Gillean, urging his mount forward. "This is the day of the Father. May his might and fury bring justice upon the earth. And may I be his swift and terrible sword."

Chapter Forty-two
The Casualty

The gathering storm showed no sign of clearing. If anything, the sky became more unsettling with each passing minute. Its swollen clouds had increased, growing darker, angrier, churning and billowing out in fists of black and ghoulish green. It was what the people of Odaunta called "a wailing sky"; for since the world had fallen, storms such as this had swept away entire towns. Normally, they would all be taking shelter, but not today. There was more than one type of storm brewing against the mountains.

Ahead, they could see the cliffs which marked their destination. These stood straight and tall beneath the shadow. Above them, the peaks of Akros jutted upward like dragon's teeth. The winds were against them here. The gusts were soundless, yet cold as ice. They carried with them a most foul and sickening smell. Though it may have puzzled some of the folk, Gillean knew it well. It was the smell of a battlefield. It was making the horses restless, yet there was little they could do about that. It would not be much farther.

All at once, Gillean saw it: the field from his dream. It was laid wide before them, almost as wide as the sea, or so it seemed. Yet now, it was different. The peculiar plants were gone, burned to ash by some mighty conflagration. It had occurred recently. The scorched ground still smelled like smoke. The eyes of the people grew wide and fearful, yet still they remained undaunted. They followed Gillean out across the charred expanse, quietly comforting their horses as they went.

"Hush now, not a word," commanded Gillean in a voice that was soft but firm. "Pass the message along to those behind. From this point on, we need to keep silent."

'Ere long, the burnt ground began to swell steadily upwards. It peaked just ahead of them in a broad slope, obscuring their vision like the roll of a rising wave.

What lay beyond this point? Would they have the thorny wood to provide them cover, or had that, too, been burned? Something in Gillean's gut told him that it had. When they crested that hill, he knew, there would be nothing between them and the terror which waited at the gates. This fact was firmly rooted in his mind like a weed, as sure as the sun no longer shown.

Gillean dismounted and drew one of his revolvers. From beyond the slope, he could hear the buzzing of flies and a thousand other parasites. He signaled to the townspeople (his troops) to make ready their weapons. The foul wind was a knife cutting across his face.

Gillean could lead a blind charge as well as any other man, yet it was entirely against his instincts. *I doubt that's what you're expecting of me,* he thought, *to lead them over this hill into an ambush and have them all shot up and torn to bits.*

He needed to know exactly what they were up against. Avira wanted to accompany him, but he waved her back. This he must do alone.

He moved swiftly, hunched over like an ape. When he neared the top, he dropped to his belly and crawled. Gillean could feel the pent-up breath of the townspeople as they watched and waited. It was a tension most unique. It was painful, like bleeding fingers snagged against a wire strand.

Ever so cautiously, Gillean raised his head and surveyed the scene before him. He had been correct. There was no black and thorny wood. Instead, he saw a sea of decaying bodies. They littered the ground, ringed in an enormous semi-circle, stretching almost to the gates themselves. Each and every corpse lay prostrate, as if they had all died praying. If the stench had been bad before, now it was horrendous, a repulsive reek which nearly took away his breath.

How had all these people come to perish here? Were they seeking the same as he? Had they attempted a stand against evil? Somehow, he doubted it. At any rate, Gillean did not have time to wonder long.

In the deepening shadow beneath the glowering, cliff-walled gates, dark-robed figures swayed with the rancid wind. Gillean peered closer and realized that they were all young men and women, some of them seemingly no more than teens. These were the students of Arius, those stolen in the night for service to the Assembly. He did not know if they were armed. They did not appear to be, but that was no indication. Those in the service of the cursed laurels were seldom without weapons.

They were gathered around about a cluster of ruins, focusing on what seemed to be a large reddish-brown rock. Yet, as Gillean continued to stare, he realized that it was not a rock at all. It was the creature from the church at Gaven post. It was the tamandua. The thing had them under its spell.

Even as Gillean's blood began to rise, he could hear the still, small voice inside his soul. It was cautioning him, warning him to wait; yet it did not have his attention. His mind was divided between the movements of the demon and his ever-growing anger. His heart was afflicted with the memories of his friend and a certain valley of forgotten bones. Gillean was now sure of why he had come. There was not a doubt in his mind, and he had already determined what he was going to do. He was ready to bring this whole thing to an end.

Thoughtless and furious with rage, he rose up from concealment. Before he even knew what he was doing, he found himself running, bounding down the other side of the slope. Alerted by his movements, the townspeople sprang to life and charged after him.

Gillean leapt over the bodies. They were nothing to him, just the shells of fools now souless in the void. He moved like lightning. As he raised his revolver, the young people looked up at him; their faces vacant and expressionless, their eyes lost in some other world.

Gillean was quick, yet the tamandua was quicker. As Gillean took aim at him, he grabbed hold of a young man, using him as a shield. Gillean could hear Avira's voice screaming behind him, yet it was too late. He had already pulled the trigger.

There was a crack of lightning and a boom as thunder smacked the air. The boy's eyes widened and glazed as dark blood erupted from the front of his robe. The tamandua gave a haunting cackle as it leapt away. Gillean hated himself for what he had just done, yet he could not stop now. He fired again and again at the fleeing beast. It darted and dodged with supernatural speed, yet one of the shots winged it and sent it sprawling.

Gillean moved advanced on his fallen foe with undiluted hatred in his eyes. With one fluid motion, he drew his sword. The world around was a dream to him now, an illusion for which he had no time. This was his purpose, his true and violent need; to ensure this creature's death, and if possible, its utter destruction. Yet, before he could take another step, a group of riders galloped past him, nearly bowling him over. In the instant before the stamping hooves crushed the creature, it gave him a sadistic smile. Its charcoal eyes twinkled at the moment of its death as to say, "see you next go round."

In a daze, Gillean turned back to face the dark-robed youth, unoffended that he had almost been run over. The first person he saw was Avira. She was kneeling on the broken stones, holding the boy he had shot. His already pale face had become almost completely white. His mother had tried to staunch the crimson flow from his chest, but to no avail. As she wept, he raised his face to look at her and the light of recognition lit his dimming eyes. For the first time in what must have been an eternity, he smiled.

As the young man choked out his final breath, Gillean turned away. He could just picture the look on Avira's face. He could also imagine the way she would look at him hence forth and forever. Even as godly as she was, a part of her would always hate him. Nothing could undo that. The Father had promised her her son, and he, Gillean, had taken him away again. He had become a murderer.

The horses and riders clopped and stumbled about as the sounds of sobbing slowed and died. The newly liberated youth sat with their fallen comrade and his mother. They seemed confused, still trying to make sense of what had just happened. Slowly, the boy's two sisters approached to comfort their mother. Their movements were still, at first, numb and mechanical. Yet, as she embraced them, they began to feel again and cried with her, their tears every bit as sincere as hers. She kissed their faces and they cried more.

Other citizens of Odaunta began venture forward. Approaching the young people, they scanned the faces for any hint of their long lost relatives, and miracle of miracles, they began to find them. There was sobbing mixed with laughter. Everyone began to talk at once. For many, it was as if their children and grandchildren had been called back from the grave.

Gillean knew he had to get them out of here; yet, at the same time, he knew their work was not done. Had this mangy demonic beast been the reason for their march on Akron? God forbid. Where was the true terror, the enormous monster which had haunted his thoughts ever since he had first dreamed of its existence?

As if in answer to his thoughts there was a low, guttural rumbling from the gates. The people lifted their eyes in unison, their expressions were anything but brave. One might have thought that giving them back their children would have increased their courage and will to live, but there was something about this place. Others had said as much. There was just something about the gates of Akron, something that weakened the bones.

"Pick up your weapons!" he shouted. Get these children back over the wall (he doubted they would mind being called children just now). If you want to save them, we need to cover their escape. Let's do what we came here to do!"

Even as he spoke, the ground spoke and a dark thing came lurching passed the narrow gates. As the rain came rushing down, its red eyes burned like molten jasper. It was more terrible than anything Gillean, or the old people could have ever imagined.

Chapter Forty-three:
Battle at the Gates

A toothy maw ready and willing to swallow up the world. This was what Gillean saw as he stared down the monster. Yes, he was afraid, but there was more to it than that. His heart was made a seething pot, not just from anxiety and terror, but from rage and grief, as well as his overwhelming sense of duty: duty to the Father as well as to all who lived and breathed. This creature, this fiendish, reptilian monster was a servant of death. Hell followed with it. He could feel its wretched heat and torment emanating from the creature's charred, black skin. The monster must be destroyed for the good of all.

He did not rejoice that he was the one appointed. On the contrary, he shuddered at what he must do. It was a task which would most certainly claim his life, yet, he had been led unto it by the Father; and if the Father was for him...

Another groaning, guttural cry, cut off his thoughts. The time for pondering was past. In the pouring rain, he leapt atop the crumbling ruins. As he did, Gillean called out to the Father.

"Lord, give me strength and quickness; the wisdom needed to bring down this beast. Teach my hands to war and my fingers to fight."

He drew first one revolver, then another. The shots burst forth in timed succession, aimed for the monster's glowing eyes. The beast roared as the bullets struck home. They punched through sending showers of black blood to mingle with the rain. But the terror would not be defeated so easily. With a shuddering howl, its form melted into smoke and it divided into its subsequent parts: a cat, a snake, an owl, and a wolf.

The people of Odaunta, opened up with their weapons. Some shouted prayers and hexes, others spoke the name of the Father, forcefully as they shot. Somehow, they seemed to have overcome their fear.

For a moment, the demonic creatures just stood there seemingly unaffected by the hail of bullets. Then, with a scream which would haunt Gillean until his dying day, they rushed the townspeople. Bodies flew through the air. The cries of men and women mingled with hisses and howls. There was blood and the pounding of horse's hooves as man raged against monster, and many lost their lives.

Gillean took aim at the snake, he could see it writhing, undulating as it tried to get at him. It swung sideways, snapping a man's neck with its tail. Praying, he squeezed the trigger and put a bullet through its head.

Next, he turned his attention to the cat. It was darting to and fro, toppling anyone it could. With its sharp teeth it tore at men's necks, bathing itself in blood. He shot at it, missed, and fired again. The ocelot was quick, yet not quick enough to evade the slashing hoof of one of the horses. The blow sent it flying, and Gillean shot it in mid-air, and it exploded in a mess of fur and ashen dust.

As far as he could tell, none of the creatures he killed were reanimating. He was thankful, yet not overly confident that they would remain dead. They were demons after all. The Father would have to restrain them, yet would He?

Suddenly there was a cry from the charred slope behind them. More men and women came charging towards them, brandishing rifles and bows. At the same time, the narrow gates came alive with Mavarians. They cackled and hooted, raising their weapons to meet the onslaught. Gillean and his force were caught in the middle.

"Everyone! Get down!" he screamed, throwing himself flat, and not a moment too soon. The two sides opened up on each other like children in a shooting gallery. Their pattern of fire was disorganized, yet enough of the shots hit their marks. The villagers and hill people fell, their bodies littering the slope with those of the dead worshipers. Some of the Mavarians fell as well, yet not nearly as many. Most had body armor and seemingly no fear of death. They pressed their advantage charging forward, their rapid-fire weapons blazing as they went.

Just when Gillean thought it wall all over, a voice boomed out from somewhere up above. "A thousand shall fall at thy right hand, yet it shall not come nigh thee!"

Suddenly, the shooting stopped. The Mavarians faltered. Their weapons had all jammed and they seemed to have lost their focus.

Before they had the change to react further, Gillean was on his feet again, firing like a madman. The bullets flew through them like hot knives through butter. Clouds of fur and feathers filled the soaked air as he assailed them. Some stumbled back to try and run, but ended up falling and being trampled by their compatriots.

Gillean paused to reload two of his revolvers, but had no more time before they were on him again, surrounding him endeavoring to bring him down. He punched through them with his remaining fourteen shots, then, pulled out his long-bladed daggers. He spun and danced through them with at a feverish pace. He leapt like a deer, knocking them over and slashing as he went. His body was a living weapon and he could feel the power of God flowing through him. Gillean discovered that every time he even touched a Mavarian, it crumpled as if hit with a sledgehammer. This had to be the Father. He could conceive of no other explanation.

Suddenly, he felt a burning pain tear through his arms. Cruel gripping claws cut into his shoulders, yanking him off his feet and dragging him into the air. The great owl had a hold of him. Its wings beat hard, bludgeoning his head. A trickle of blood ran from his nose and down his chin. There was a feeling of utter helplessness, icy despair as the talons dug deeper, ripping through the tissue and into the bone.

Gillean was in agony. He could sense the demon was mocking him, its rasping voice twisting in a gargling, hissing laughter. He could see the eyes of the wolf, snarling up at him. It was watching, waiting for his fall. When it came, the beast would lunge upon him to devour what was left.

He sensed the owl wanted him to drop his weapons. For a moment more he resisted, fighting back in his mind and continuing to call out to the Father, then the tamandua leapt upon him. The added weight sent a new burst of fire through his limbs. He sensed his arms were about to be ripped from his body.

The red-furred creature leaned in towards his ear, its cold breath sending shivers down his spine. "You do know, we can never really die...unlike you," the demon chortled. "You have fought a good fight, now let us end this futile game. Curse your god and die!"

"You can be the one to die!" Gillean gasped. His lungs felt as if they were filling up with fire and blood. "In the name of the Father, and of Jesus, depart from me!"

"You really think that will work for you here? Here and now? This is our stronghold, and besides, it looks like someone needs to reevaluate his relationship with the Father. Only those who walk closely with Him can have authority over us. You fool. You should have listened to His spirit when you had the chance, now you must despair!"

The creatures all screamed at once. The sound cut into Gillean's nerves just as the talons cut his flesh and bone. He wanted to scream with them, yet was unable. The snake had wrapped itself about his neck.

Just when he thought death had found him, Gillean saw a bright and brilliant light. It burst forth above his head, making the demon owl shriek and flutter backwards. Then he was falling, falling fast, his wounds burning as if clutched by flaming pincers. There was fire all about him now, it burned white-hot and he was sure he it would consume him. Yet the only places which it touched were the spots in which he had been wounded. Pure flame, unlike any he had ever seen. Suddenly he knew, it was of the Father. It had been sent to make him clean.

Gillean's landing was anything but gentle, yet he survived. His fall was broken by a cluster of dazed Mavarias. The impact of his body broke each and every one of their necks.

Looking up, Gillean tried to determine the source of the white flames. They still arched above his head, rushing in a torrent which seemed to permeate every drop of rain. In another moment it had subsided. Once again, the world was dark and cold, but not completely. There remained one light, one last remnant of the sacred fire. It came from a man all dressed in white. He was tall and strong and in his hand he held a burning sword.

As soon as he caught sight of him, Gillean realized he had seen this man before. He had come to is rescue years ago, when the one called Hector had endeavored to remove his heart. Gillean had known him as Sammy, yet now, he had the feeling the man's name might very well be something else. *Samuel perhaps?* It sounded right, but Gillean did not dare address him. He was truly magnificent, a fearful sight. This was a messenger from the Father and he was more powerful and terrible than the beast or any of the demons could dream of being.

"Take heed all ye who are on this earth," the voice was like resonant thunder. "The days have come for the trying of thy faith. Soon, and very soon, this world shall be set alight. Soon, and very soon, all things great and small shall be called into account. I have been summoned and charged with rebuking those who are at enmity with the Father. Evil must needs continue for a time; yet today, a fire shall be kindled, and this world shall be left without excuse. Behold the rebuke of the Lord!"

With this, the angel raised his flaming sword. There was a mighty rush of wind, the aura of ozone and broken bones cast upon a pyre. All the world seemed to be holding its final breath.

The last thing Gillean could recall was a face both beautiful and sad. It was the lovely Ameara, his Ameara, the one for whom he longed. She looked down at him as if from some great height, her blue eyes more brilliant and pure than ever before; yet, she was not smiling. She looked to be consumed by grief. Why was she grieving? Was it...for him? Gillean reached for her, but lost her all the same. The vision faded and reality swung in upon him with an unimaginable vengeance.

The angel smote the earth with his flaming sword, and all was flung into oblivion. For a moment of sheer and indescribable terror, there was no world; then Gillean Weaver, the last surviving soul of the battle of Akron, succumbed to forces far beyond his control and was claimed by darkness.

Conclusion:

Somewhere between the world that was and the world that now lies dying, a mausoleum is repaired. Its cracks are sealed and its vine-covered walls made as new. Inside, in the dank and musty darkness, five beasts wait their next release.

Their master is a patient creature, though unspeakably evil, a worker of guile and vice. He is a master of shadows and deceiver of nations, yet even he must answer for his deeds in time to come. When shall he return to bid the beasts be loosed again? Who can say?

Until then, they shall abide, thinking their evil thoughts and dreaming, dreaming of the days when their wanton havoc raped the world of man. If they sleep forever, it will not be too long, yet something tells me they shall be loosed again, and soon. Soon, and very soon, we shall see them going about their father's business.

But wait, something has changed. The ground beneath the mausoleum has begun to quiver, to shake with the tremors of some hidden force, some great and malicious, hidden power. And by this happening, the very foundations of that place are thrown asunder.

A fissure appears and the earth is opened. The hexagon is swallowed up. Down, down, down it falls, spinning like a child's top, or a casket lost to the deep.

As it descends into the blackness, it takes on the appearance of an eye. The sallow white of the marble glimmers with the last rays of a dying light. It seems morbidly cheerful, as if to say, "So long for now, friend. See you next go round."

When Gillean awoke, the air was filled with floating ash. The bodies were gone, wiped from the face of the earth. The Gates of Akron lay collapsed, impassable. There was nothing living here save for him. The realization was a fearful one, causing him to feel weak and hollow inside. There was no sign of Samuel, aside from the damage he had inflicted.

In the gray and dusty haze, Gillean Weaver lifted up his eyes. Somewhere far above, past the clouds and billows of ash, a distant orb was glowing. It was cold and weak, yet there it was. For the first time in nearly seven years, the sun was attempting to shine.

The End

Made in the
USA
Columbia, SC